I0552759

# THE ROAD TO FROSTY HOLLOW

RJ SCOTT

MEREDITH RUSSELL

# The Road to Frosty Hollow

Copyright © 2016 RJ Scott and Meredith Russell

Cover design by Meredith Russell, Edited by Sue Adams

This edition Copyright © 2024 RJ Scott and Meredith Russell

ISBN: 9781785645563

Published by Love Lane Books

## Dedication

*For our family and friends, and everyone who loves Christmas.*

# THE ROAD TO *Frosty* HOLLOW

RJ SCOTT & MEREDITH RUSSELL

# Chapter One

"THIS IS CRAZY, SIS. I CAN'T BELIEVE I LET YOU TALK ME into this road trip."

Nick Sheridan sat on the end of the bed and stared at his luggage. He'd been pacing a line back and forth in front of his bedroom window for what felt like hours, but, was really only minutes, and his nerves were getting the better of him. He held his cell phone in front of him, set on speakerphone, waiting for the reassuring sound of his sister's voice to fill the room.

"It'll do you good. It'll do you and Cameron both some good," Kaitlin said.

Her voice held an edge of excitement. She was setting him up, and he knew it, and he was pretty sure she knew he knew it. Cameron Bennett was the last person Nick wanted to share a cross-country drive with, with his dimples, and his smile and his ability to make Nick forget how to speak.

With a sigh, he scratched a hand though his hair, teasing his bangs to spiky points. "Maybe." He glanced around his bedroom. He was supposed to have packed everything into boxes ready for the move back home in the New Year, but surfaces were still scattered with mementos of his life and his closet remained full of his clothes.

Kaitlin asked, "What time did Cameron say he was getting there?"

Nick rested his phone on the bed and got to his feet. "Anytime now." He crossed to the window. Lifting a slat in the blind, he looked out on the street below.

Kaitlin's voice came from the bed behind him. "You remember what he looks like, right?"

How could he not remember Cameron Bennett? The man's face was plastered all over his sister's social media every time Cam happened to be in the same state as her: Cam and Kaitlin horseback riding along a treacherous mountain trail, or jumping out of a plane, or parasailing. The man took risks that made Nick worry, considering Kaitlin sometimes got involved too. Kaitlin and Cameron had been best friends since any of them could remember.

Not only that, but Cameron's face was all wrapped up in memories of one stolen kiss and years of what ifs.

Not that he was admitting that to his sister. "Shut up," he said, raising his voice to make sure she could hear him.

Kaitlin laughed. "It's so easy to wind you up. But seriously, have some fun, live life, get all thinky about what you want to do."

"*Thinky*?" Nick mouthed the word to the room and smiled. He *had* been thinking. In fact, he'd done nothing but thinking ever since he received the official invitation to Kaitlin's wedding a few months ago.

Sitting on his dresser was the ivory-and-turquoise-decorated card. Nick eyed the names of his sister and soon-to-be brother-in-law, struck by a strange sense of loss. He rubbed at the feeling of emptiness in his stomach. When he had settled in Seattle two-and-a-half years ago, he'd thought that was it. Sure, there might have been a chance he would be called back to active duty, but Seattle had felt like home. He'd had a boyfriend and the promise of a career and finishing up school. It had been a fresh start. True, he and his family lived on opposite sides of the country, but that was okay; he had things to work through, and they didn't need a screwed-up Marine in their lives.

Now, of course, the boyfriend was no more, the career was at a grinding halt, and he'd failed his last exam. *Yeah, life's great.*

"Nick? You still there?"

Nick breathed in deeply and glanced over his shoulder at his phone. "I'm here."

Now he was in need of another fresh start, and as far as he was concerned, running back to his hometown in Vermont was for the best. He needed the security of having his family around him, at least for a while until he got his head on straight.

*Then why haven't you packed yet?*

"I have to go," Kaitlin interrupted his thoughts. "I've got an appointment with the florist. Mom's coming with me, so wish me luck."

Their mom had taken to the role of mother of the bride like it was a military campaign. Kaitlin had even taken the drastic measure of phoning Nick one night, stressed, cursing, and insisting their mom should have signed up with him eight years ago. It was kind of nice she reached out to him, as though he was needed. "So, I'll wish you a safe journey, big brother, and guess I'll see you in three weeks. Text me, right? Text me a lot. Photos as well."

Yeah, right. Photos of Cameron and his broad, stupid smile and his hazel eyes, standing next to Nick, the battered former Marine. Those were photos she'd love to share on her Facebook page. No way that was happening.

"Three weeks," he confirmed.

Then he shook his head, even though no one could see him. That was a long time to be just him and Cameron. He yawned widely. He'd not slept properly last night; when he'd rolled over on his arm, discomfort had kept him awake.

"Like I said, it'll be good for you. Just—" She paused for a moment. "—just enjoy the ride and see where it takes you."

Nick chewed his lip. His life had been so regimented throughout his twenties, and though he was all for living in the moment and taking some chances, his default setting was survival and it was difficult to adjust. "I'll try."

"See that you do. Anyway, I have to go. Feel free to give Cam a big hug from me." Her voice held a laugh as she teased him.

Shaking his head, he picked up his phone. "Later, sis."

"Love you."

"You too." He ended the call and pocketed his phone.

Blowing out a breath, he checked around the room. Everything he'd put on his list was packed in his case and large backpack. He had three weeks on the road and an undetermined amount of time with his folks for the wedding, Christmas, and into next year.

His cell phone chimed and he freed it once more from

his pocket and eyed the details of the text message. It was from Cameron.

*Getting gas. Be with you in ten.*

*OK*, he typed.

He hesitated, wondering if he was supposed to say more. Billy, his ex, added smiley faces to all his texts, even when he was pissed. "I am so out of the loop," he muttered. With a shrug, he hit Send; he didn't want to give Cameron a weird message by using the wrong yellow faces.

"Okay," he said to his room. "This is really happening."

When Kaitlin had suggested he join Cameron on his road trip from Seattle to Vermont, Nick's first instinct had been to say no.

He remembered a lot about Cameron; his illness as a kid that kept him in his room a lot, his stupidly cute hair, his thoughtful expressions. And the kiss. He recalled the kiss and Cameron pushing him away in great detail.

But they weren't friends like Cameron and Kaitlin were. Being two years older than them meant Nick had always been a step ahead in the checkpoints of life— graduating, going away to college, dropping out to embark on a career in the military.

*Not anymore. Hell, you're going backward.* It was as though his life had been unraveling over the last five months. His relationship had ended, he wasn't happy at work, and he had no direction, no damn idea what to do with himself.

*At least being a Marine gave you stability and focus.*

It had given him other things too. He glanced down at the palm of his hand, then curled his fingers, brushing the faded scars that stretched down to his wrist. The memory of gunfire made his shoulders tense, and just for a moment he was back there, his patrol under attack, and jagged rocks shredding his hand as he scrambled for cover.

The idea to re-enlist had been a brief one, some knee-jerk reaction to change in his life. But he soon changed his mind; he had done his time, served his country. He wasn't a career soldier. He needed something else. If only he could figure out what that was....

Shaking off the old memories, Nick took the few minutes he had to check over his luggage and the apartment. There was a feeling of unease as he picked up the wedding invitation. In three weeks he would be back in Vermont, back in Frosty Hollow. He hadn't been home since Christmas two years ago, and that had been a flying visit.

The sound of the intercom buzzer interrupted his thoughts. *Too late to change your mind now.*

He paused at the receiver, his hand hovering over the speak button. The buzzer rang again and Nick took a breath. "Okay," he said to himself, then pressed the button and spoke into the intercom. "I'll be right down."

After gathering his things, he checked the apartment one last time before heading downstairs. He pushed open the building door with his shoulder and backed outside, turning around to maneuver his belongings through the door with him.

"You need a hand?"

He stopped. The door swung shut behind him. "What?" It took him a moment to link the voice to the man standing at the bottom of the short flight of steps leading up to the apartment building. Tall and wide across the chest, with stubble and sunglasses pushed back in his hair, Cameron Bennett looked like a cross between a biker and a model, and he was every bit as gorgeous in person as Nick remembered. He looked a bit pale, white against the dark of his jacket, but hell, he looked good.

Cameron removed his shades, folded down the arms, and nodded toward Nick's suitcase. "Your things. Do you need any help with them?"

Lifting his pack higher on his shoulder, Nick shook his head. "I'm good. Thanks."

When Nick didn't move, Cameron raised one of his neat eyebrows. "What?" he asked with a smile, shifting his weight onto his other leg and looking up at Nick expectantly. "I got something on my face?" His smile widened. The way Cameron's lips curled made dimples appear in his face. Yep, there they were, the Dimples of Doom.

"What? No, sorry." Nick lowered his head. "I just…." He looked Cameron up and down. *Cameron Bennett all grown up.* "I was trying to remember how long it's been." He picked up his suitcase and headed down to the sidewalk, where he met Cameron's hazel eyes and waited for an answer.

"Nine or ten years, I guess." Cameron walked behind him. "Senior year, wasn't it? My senior year, anyway. You'd come home from college for the weekend, and Kaitlin had that Valentine's party."

Nick didn't have to try to remember the party, ever since he'd agreed to this road trip he'd had the damn party on his mind. He didn't want to talk about it, not after making a fool of himself with Cameron, thinking the other man actually wanted to kiss him. But Cameron was looking at him expectantly; waiting for an answer.

"*Alice in Wonderland*," he said, finally. Kaitlin had roped him into decorating the house with strings of hearts and playing cards.

And he and Cameron had kissed. *Don't think about the kiss.*

"I'm impressed you even remember. You were pretty drunk." Cameron grinned. It didn't look like Cameron recalled the kiss, or the awkwardness that followed it.

"A house full of Mad Hatters is enough to drive anyone to drink." Nick offered; anything to stop thinking on things that should never have happened. The party had been the night after he'd come out to his parents and told them he was dropping out of college to enlist all in one go. Turned out him being gay wasn't a problem to his parents. Signing up, however, they hadn't taken too well. Not at first, anyway.

"So many sexy Cheshire Cats and slutty Alice's," Cameron mused.

Nick prodded Cameron in the back. "Hey, my sister was Alice. She wasn't slutty." He couldn't help the defensiveness that stiffened his spine.

"Nicky, I'm kidding."

*Nicky.* The name surprised him. He hadn't been called that in years. Even his sister had dropped the cutesy version of his name.

If Cameron noticed Nick's faltering steps, he didn't make it evident. Instead he continued. "Seriously, I'm the last person to judge anyone for what they wear." Cameron spun around, walking backward a few steps as he tugged at the front of the V-necked T-shirt he wore under a leather jacket. The action exposed more of his chest.

Nick noted the faint dusting of hair across the pale skin of Cameron's chest and what looked like the edge of a tattoo.

"My name is Nick, not Nicky."

Cameron nodded his understanding, and with a smile, he slid his shades back on and stepped out into the street.

They stopped by a functional black SUV with snow tires and Nick blinked to make sure he wasn't seeing things. "Thought you were a muscle car fan? This isn't quite what I imagined for your grand cross-country adventure."

Cameron pulled open the driver side door and rested his arms on top of the frame. He shrugged as he looked over the roof of the black SUV, meeting Nick's eyes. "Well, I had considered renting a Mustang, maybe. But then I remembered it's December and we have snow."

"Good call."

"Anyway, I know you like working with cars, but I didn't want you having a busman's holiday every time we broke down."

"Thoughtful of you." Nick was aiming for jokey, but he sounded more sarcastic than joking.

Cameron looked confused at the tone and he worried at his lip for a moment. "You *can* still change your mind, you know. I won't be offended."

"About what?"

"The road trip, three weeks with me. I know Kaitlin can be very persuasive when she wants to be."

Shaking his head, Nick said, "She can be, but I want to do this." He might have been quick to blame Kaitlin for the road trip, but he was really doing it for himself. "I promise you this is my decision."

Cameron seemed to consider Nick's words as he tapped the fingers of one hand on the back of the other. "Okay." He pulled the door open a little farther. "Put your things in the back and we'll get out of here."

After loading his bags in the trunk, Nick slipped into the car and strapped himself in beside Cameron. "So, what's the plan?"

"Spokane."

"Sorry?" He raised an eyebrow.

"That's where we're headed, or at least we are, according to Kaitlin. It's just over five hours from here." Cameron reached behind the passenger seat and pulled out a map. "Figured we could drive a couple of hours, stop for something to eat at the halfway point, and then do the rest."

"What the hell's in Spokane?" Nick asked. "Kaitlin picked the place?"

Cameron looked sheepish. "She may have planned the whole trip. Well, I mean, I helped and all, but she was the one who came up with the itinerary."

"Right. Okay." Nick scratched behind his ear.

"Here." Cameron opened the glove compartment and pulled out a notebook. Loose, folded sheets of paper stuck out from between the pages. "I printed off what we decided on."

Nick folded back the corner of the little book, allowing the paper to flick across his thumb as he slowly released the pages. He rested it on top of the map across his thighs. "I know you asked me about wanting to do this, but are you okay with me being here?"

It seemed Kaitlin had a much bigger role in the trip than Nick first thought, but he wasn't entirely sure about Cameron's reasons for taking the cross-country trip. Apparently, it was some mix of a personal work project and self-evaluation of his life.

Cameron curled his hands around the steering wheel. "Trust me. You'd know if I didn't want you here." He briefly turned to look at Nick. "And you never know—we might actually have some fun."

With a nod, Nick agreed, "Yeah, we might."

"So," Cameron said. "Ready?"

*As I'll ever be.* "Sure. Let's do it."

After all, how bad could three weeks on the road with Cameron be?

## Chapter Two

NICK HAD TWO CDs IN HIS HAND. THE ONES THAT HAD been on the passenger seat, if Cameron recalled correctly. Queen's *Greatest Hits* and the latest Beyoncé album. "You can choose," he said.

Nick seemed lost in thought, tapping a finger on the CD cases, his brow furrowed and his lips thinned. Wordlessly, he passed the Queen CD to Cameron and placed the other one into the glove box. Cameron started the music; it dipped to silent when he turned the engine on. Then the strains of *Bohemian Rhapsody* filled the cabin and he smiled, more to himself than Nick. Cameron had talked about the party but hadn't mentioned the kiss, and neither had Nick. He was happy to pretend it hadn't happened so they never spoke of it again.

NICK HAD FOLLOWED *him out of the party, and onto the wide verandah.*

*"Hey, why you out here?" Nick had asked. "Is everything okay?"*

*"It's all just too much," Cameron had replied, with honesty. He was hot and tired and the music was too loud, not to mention Kaitlin was in there sucking face with a guy and he no longer had his best friend as his wing man.*

*Pity flooded Nick's expression, and he'd stepped close. "Must be hard getting used to the chaos outside your room."*

*Cameron hadn't had an answer to that, just offered a simple, "yeah."*

*Then it happened.*

*"Can I try something to make you smile?" That was all Nick said. Nick feeling sorry for him. Nick cradling his face.*

*Nick kissing him.*

THE KISS HAD BEEN hot and sexy and frightening all at the same time. But it had only happened because Nick felt sorry for the sick kid at his first real party. In his shame and embarrassment Cameron pushed Nick away, then ran.

Nick hadn't followed him, or called him, or spoken of it again. Then of course he'd gone and signed up and left Frosty Hollow soon after.

No point in bringing the kiss up, or Nick's choice to sign up, or his leaving or, in fact, anything serious.

"So, Spokane," Nick murmured, and his words pulled Cameron out of the twist of memories that had him quiet.

Cameron cleared his throat. "Yeah, thought we'd go the scenic route, stay off the main roads. You okay with that?"

Nick nodded but didn't say anything, so Cameron assumed it was a done deal. He consulted the notes Kaitlin had sent through after their skyping session and typed in the first zip code that was in Leavenworth.

Nick watched his actions, then asked, "What's there?"

"Lunch, some place Kaitlin found, does the best Bavarian sausage or something." Cameron concentrated on making sure the navigation system was guiding them northeast of the city as opposed to southeast and the freeways, and then he pulled away from Nick's place. "Nice area you live in," he said, just because he wanted to say something.

Nick made a noise somewhere in the region of a yes, but it was more growl than word. Cameron could have pushed for more detail, but Kaitlin had mentioned her brother was moving away from this apartment, although she didn't elaborate why. Maybe Nick hated it here, so no point in rocking the boat. She also mentioned he was considering making Vermont his permanent home, but that was all Cameron knew about him, other than he was now officially a former Marine and was looking for the next stage in his life.

Must be hard on the guys who leave the forces only to find that the world they left behind had moved on without them. Nick looked good, though—but then, he always had. There was an edge to Nick, a roughness and strength fueling quite a few of Cameron's teenage fantasies. Even more so when Nick had come out to his parents in the same conversation where he said he was signing up to be a Marine.

Never let it be said that Nick did things by halves.

They made it out of the city in good time. At a couple

of points, Nick was humming along with the songs on the CD, but after an hour, when Cameron glanced over, he'd fallen asleep, dozing awkwardly in his seat. He couldn't be comfortable, and for a few moments Cameron considered poking him awake, but he'd be the first to admit that Nick had looked tired this morning.

In fact, Cameron had noticed a lot in the short time they'd talked. After all, this was Nicky, the same man who showed him how to throw a baseball, how to field a goal, how to lace his skates… and how to kiss another man.

Not that Nicky appeared to remember that.

Mentioning the party had been something Cameron promised himself he wouldn't do, and what happened? Two minutes in Nick's company and he was blurting out crap about the Wonderland party. Not that Nick had turned around and said, "Oh yeah, you remember Cameron, how I pressed you up against the wall and gave you the kiss of your young life. And then you pushed me away and I never followed you when you ran."

Of course, Nick hadn't said anything like that at all— he had just gotten defensive over his sister. *Nothing has changed*, Cameron suspected, and likely Nick didn't even recall the kiss. After all, he had been drinking.

Cameron shifted in his seat, the general ache he had in his muscles a stark reminder of the fears he was pushing way down inside him. He had a low level of fatigue that dogged his every step, and sometimes it tipped over into a feeling of weakness. He wasn't even going to think about being ill again; couldn't do that, because he didn't want to live in fear.

He set the CD to repeat and only stopped when he reached the restaurant. München Haus was in

Leavenworth. Unremarkable from the outside, it was, however, bedecked with huge plastic LED snowflakes for the season, which Cameron guessed might look quite nice in the dark, but in the daylight all the draping wires undermined any prettying effort.

"We're here," he murmured so that he wouldn't surprise Nick awake. But Nick didn't stir; he hadn't moved even when the car stopped. "Nicky," he said a little louder.

At first it didn't appear to work again, so he poked him gently in the side, and in flurry of motion, Nick woke up, his eyes wide and fixed firmly on Cameron.

"Wha—?" he asked. His level of coherence was still in sleep mode, and there was something incredibly sexy about his unfocused dark gaze as he blinked at Cameron.

"We're here," Cameron said again and indicated out the window.

Nick covered a yawn before fumbling at unbuckling his seatbelt and opening the passenger's door. With one foot on the icy ground, and a rush of cold filling the space in the car, he waited expectantly when he realized Cameron hadn't moved. "What?" he asked, sounding way more awake.

"Is this place okay? I know it was on your sister's list, but it looks—" *Tacky, run-down, a little open to the elements.*

Nick glanced at the building. "Yeah, if Kaitlin chose it, it's fine with me."

They went into the restaurant and were seated next to a huge display of children's coloring sheets featuring grinning Santas. Cameron pulled the menus over. A waitress, Sandra by her name tag, sashayed over, filled water glasses, and reeled off a list of specials. She left them to give them time to figure out their order.

Cameron couldn't handle another hour of not talking. "So, cranberry," he began, poking at the menu. "I bet as soon as Thanksgiving is done, chefs all over the US are all 'Yay, it's Christmas. Let's add cranberry to a dish and charge an extra five dollars.' " He was trying for jokey, but Nick looked up from his menu with a confused expression and then stared at Cameron as though he was growing horns.

"Sorry? What?"

"Cranberry," Cameron said weakly. "In sausages. That's what the server said, right?" He looked back down at the festive menu.

"Yep, and cranberry bread and sauce, and I think she even mentioned cranberry pancakes."

"Why do that? Is it like there's an arbitrary date when cranberry gets added to everything? They do that at Halloween as well."

"Add cranberries?"

Poor Nick looked even more confused. "No, pumpkin spice latte, pumpkin bread, pumpkin McDonald's… fuck knows, but if you eat or drink it, then it has pumpkin in it. Hell, even shower gel," he added when Nick didn't seem to want to carry on this thread of conversation. "I picked up a shower gel, and it had pumpkin in it." He pretended to shudder. "I am not having pumpkin sliding all over my body."

Nick worried his lower lip with his teeth before shutting his menu decisively. "Cranberry sausage, cranberry sauce, and a side of cranberry pancakes," he said firmly.

"Really?" Cameron couldn't help but smile.

"When in Rome," Nick offered. "Or Leavenworth, or whatever."

That was enough to kind of break the ice, and they talked a little more about Halloween. Cameron was glad they didn't move on to any other holidays, namely Valentine's, so there was no chance of going back to his mention of *the party*, an event that would forever appear in italics in Cameron's head. They ordered their food, and even though the place was packed, they were served quickly.

Nick stared down at the scarlet that filled most of his plate, as if he was worried the cranberries would stand up and walk off.

Cameron cleared his throat just as Nick forked the first of the scarlet food into his mouth. "So, tell me about what is going on with you. Your career. You're not an enlisted Marine anymore, right?"

"No," Nick said after he swallowed. Then he shook his head and focused on his plate. "Did my eight years, wasn't ready to sign up again."

Cameron waited for more details, but it seemed he would have to force Nick to talk. The taciturn Marine evidently liked his silence. Not like when they'd been at school; then, Nick had a reputation for being loud and in-your-face. Happy in his own skin, the football captain, the one who you invited to parties if you wanted them to be a success. Nick was a very easy person to fall in love with for a young, impressionable Cameron.

Added to which Kaitlin had made it her life's purpose to get him with her brother, who she was convinced was gay.

Of course, Nick hadn't come out as gay until he was leaving Frosty Hollow, but as usual, Kaitlin had been right. And her matchmaking hadn't stopped even then. She'd moved on to new men, who were *perfect* for Cameron, and every time they met up, she would "happen to" invite said men out with them.

Not one of them stuck. None were like her brother.

And then Cameron had met his first real boyfriend, Travis, all on his own, and at first he'd been proud of the fact he'd taken control of his own love life. Until Travis turned out to be an asshole.

*Should have given Kaitlin's picks more of a chance.*

Cameron soldiered on to try and break the awkward silence. "You're a mechanic, and you decided to follow that career path instead, right? That's what Kaitlin said."

"Yep, been working at a garage the last few years— temporary contracts. Couldn't take a final contract because of the possibility of being called up."

Nick sounded so matter-of-fact, but Cameron couldn't stop a shiver of unease every time he'd considered Nicky stuck in a war somewhere. "I'm glad you weren't." He winced at the single eyebrow that Nick raised in comment.

Maybe that had been the wrong thing to say. He'd spoken from the heart, but for all he knew, Nick was desperate to get back into the thick of things.

Nick didn't actually respond to that in words, though, changing the focus to what he was doing now.

"So, the guy in charge of the garage—Petey—offers me full-time, and I've been taking all these exams from the Occupational Safety and Health Administration, and he called me into the office last Tuesday and asked me how I'd done and I told him I'd just missed the math mark, and he said I needed to retake it. Which, hell, I'm a trained mechanic, but the shit they put in these workplace assessments is so damned stupid. I can figure out how to field strip a rifle with my eyes shut, fix a jeep with half an engine missing, but who the hell needs to know at what point two trains pass on a goddamn track?"

"Railroad engineers?" Cameron asked, trying to be helpful, before it clicked that Nick had asked a rhetorical question.

Nick shook his head in amusement, though, so that was something.

"Petey says then that he's reconsidered, and he was downsizing, and was I happy going to a three-day week. Maybe even two days every other. And that's not enough."

"Sounds like a bad news kind of day."

"Yeah," Nick poked at a large berry and it split and oozed on his pancake.

"So, what will you do?"

Nick looked up at him, his expression thoughtful, his brown eyes narrowed. "No idea," he finally said. "Which is why Kaitlin suggested the road trip with you, to 'get your head out of your ass and think about your life.' End of quote," he added.

"Sounds like Kaitlin. She always has a way of cutting to the chase."

They paid the check, splitting it down the middle after negotiations on whether to take turns with food or to just split everything fifty-fifty.

"You want me to drive?" Nick asked as they approached the car.

"I'm good. Don't think I won't let you share, though."

He was joking, but he'd left himself wide open to the same ridicule Kaitlin threw at him.

Nick patted the hood. "You remember the hours you'd talk about cars and movies, or cars in movies, with me when we were kids?"

Cameron recalled every single time the older Nick would sit with him in the sun room at his childhood home, talking cars, and movies, and giving Cameron the normal he craved. Not like Cameron had any other male friends; that was what missing school did to a kid. He lived a life through the movies; his window to the world denied him because of his cancer.

"I do."

"Used to be we'd chase Kaitlin out with the boredom of it, or so she said."

"She always came back with board games though, split us up."

"Yeah."

"She was a good friend," Cameron said. *And so were you, until it became more and I fell for you.*

"Anyway, I'd never come between you and your car, even when it's just a crappy rental SUV." Nick even smiled, a wide-open smile that reached his eyes, and Cameron felt instantly stupid and equal parts turned on.

Nick was a fine-looking man, all sharp angles and serious glares, but there was something hidden behind those eyes, the promise of the young guy Cameron used to know. The one who sat with the sick kid and talked cars, and played games, and didn't once make Cameron feel like it was a chore.

They spent most of the rest of the day's journey driving through the Okanogan-Wenatchee National Forest, and

Cameron concentrated on the winding roads, lost in his own thoughts. After an hour they swapped over, Cameron said it was to give Nick a chance to drive; wasn't ready to admit the fatigue that followed him around had his arms feeling like spaghetti. Nick didn't ask any questions, and at least this way Cameron got to admire the scenery. The forest was beautiful, and Cameron had a folder of photos on his computer from his last hike here. This time it wasn't hiking that had him stopping at the Quality Inn & Suites on Liberty Lake; it was a very different kind of fun.

Fun he very much intended on having. If he didn't wake up feeling dizzy like he had been lately on and off. Or weak, or short of breath.

"You okay sharing a room?" Cameron asked as he checked the itinerary. "I didn't realize Kaitlin had made them all single-room bookings."

"I'm happy if you are," Nick said after a moment's hesitation that could have meant anything. "No sense in paying for two rooms."

"Okay, then," Cameron said, just for something to say, when all he wanted to ask was if Nick was really, *completely* sure.

They booked into the room with two beds, dumped their bags, and put toiletries in the bathroom and organized a few things. Nick took longer about it, and so they met up again in the foyer.

Nick peered at the printed sheets. "What's on Kaitlin's list?"

"A zip line experience in the forest." Cameron waved the paper in front of Nick's face. "Obstacles, climbing. You up for that, Marine?"

Nick looked at him steadily, unblinking, then gave a

curt nod. What the hell had passed across his features before that? Surprise, fear, excitement? Cameron couldn't tell. But at least Nick hadn't said no.

*You have to try to get him out of his shell*, Kaitlin had told him. *He doesn't talk, prefers silence.*

Cameron had noticed all of that; the way Nick was happy to look out of the window and stare at the passing scenery. Nick wasn't the one who started conversations, and when they did talk he was the one to pulled away. The zip line tour involved less adrenaline than waiting around for the people in front to move along. Also, if Cameron got dizzy it was okay, he'd be attached to a safety wire the whole time.

*I can do this.*

The Stapleton family from Montana was there on vacation, apparently, and moving on to skiing next. Hell, by the time Nick and Cameron were halfway around the course Cameron even knew the sex habits of the Stapleton's hamster, which was not something he'd ever thought he'd learn.

Nick was biting his lip again, and Cameron imagined he was doing it to stop himself from laughing out loud.

He was also rubbing at his wrist but stopped when he realized Cameron was watching. Cameron almost asked him about it, only Mrs. Stapleton was loudly debating who should go first.

Their daughter—kind of small but very sweet—wasn't impressed with the next zip line drop because you couldn't see the other end, but at that point it was go back or go forward; there was no other way down. The mom went first, her squeal of excitement loud enough to scare any and all critters in the nearby trees. Then it was Little

Stapleton's go, and her dad was probably not the best person to be left with her. He was a blustery, confident guy and called his daughter stupid. Not to her face, not in words, but with subtle eye-rolls and tutting sounds as she hesitated to move off the stand.

Cameron wanted to smack him, and Nick simply stared, but Cameron could see a twitch at the corner of his mouth and the way his jaw was hard, his form tense.

"C'mon, Maisie," Dad Stapleton said. "You're holding people up."

"It's a long way," Maisie said back, even as her dad attached the hook to the trolley on the zip line.

Then the dad did something that in his head probably seemed like a good thing, but hell, he not so gently pushed his daughter off the platform. She screamed and then squealed. As she bounced down, far from smoothly because of the shove, she suddenly stopped. Right in the middle of the line, her hook had snagged or something.

"Give me strength," the dad said, muttering something under his breath about girls versus boys. He made to hook himself on the wire to go down after her, but Nick was there, pushing his way in front and holding up a hand.

"You go down there and your weight will knock into her and she'll go flying with an uncontrolled landing and you on top of her." Nick hooked himself onto the trolley and deliberately poked the father in the chest to get him to step back.

"And one thing, I had this marine on my team, Alice, and she was braver than a lot of men. Saved my life twice, okay. So, stop with the sexist shit."

The dad spluttered but wisely remained quiet. Cameron

didn't blame him, even from where he stood farther back, he could see the utter determination in Nick's eyes.

"Nick? What are you doing? Should we call for one of the guys in charge?" Cameron asked.

Nick shook his head. "I got this."

He pushed himself off the platform, slowly inching down, his feet up and wrapped around the wire, until he was very close to Maisie. Then he leaned over and did something clever with the wire, loosened the problem, reassuring Maisie with soft words, and finally Maisie was free and slid the rest of the way. Nick waited a little while, then followed, vanishing behind trees to presumably arrive at the platform way down below, stopped by the zip line spring braking system.

The dad was next, and he left without a word. Cameron went last. When he got to the platform, the Stapleton family were already heading out.

"Did they say thank you?" he teased.

Nick shook his head. "Maisie hugged me, but I don't need thanks."

"That was pretty heroic there."

Nick frowned again—he was doing a lot of that—and muttered something under his breath that definitely included a curse word and *hero*.

In the time it took to finish the course and get back to the hotel, with Nick rubbing at his wrist and frowning a lot, Cameron discovered Kaitlin was right. Nick was hurting, and not just physically; he'd shut himself off.

Cameron didn't think he could help, but maybe he could try, and it would make for a good project. He would forget the kiss, and the awkward shit, and focus on making Nick smile more.

After all, miracles did happen around Christmas.

## Chapter Three

"NICK? NICKY, WE'RE HERE. YOU COMING?"

Nick opened his eyes and lifted his head. He couldn't believe he'd fallen asleep again, but maybe this was his body's way of saying he needed to catch up on sleep so he could make the big decisions.

Or something equally Zen that Kaitlin would tell him.

He rubbed his jaw where he had pressed his face against the back of his fisted hand. "Where?" he asked, blinking as he sat up straight.

A cool breeze brushed his cheek. Cameron was already stepping out of the car. Nick checked the area where they'd pulled up. It was a parking lot, though he wasn't sure where they were. After what had happened with the kid and her father at the zip line, Nick hadn't wanted to talk, instead he'd chosen to turn toward the window, arm on the door, head in his hand, and close his eyes. When Maisie got stuck, he should have called the ranger or the guy in charge of the place, but he hadn't, because he worked best when he didn't think.

Cameron opened the rear door and grabbed a scarf off the back seat. He wrapped it tight, tucking it into his jacket when he pulled up the zipper, shut both doors and disappeared around the back of the SUV.

Unfastening his seatbelt, Nick stretched out his neck and gently rotated his wrist. The injury had never been enough to affect his service, but together with other knocks and shocks throughout his years of active duty, there was a deeper ache sometimes, right to his bones.

He got out, surprised by the freshness of the air, which resounded with a gentle roar as he walked to the back of the car.

"What are we doing?" He zipped up his coat and pulled up the hood. The soft brown material protected his cheeks from the cool chill encircling them.

Cameron shut the trunk of the car. Nick noted the camera he held in his hand.

"We're stepping out for some air." Cameron smiled and pressed the lock button on his key fob. The car's lights flashed.

With a raised eyebrow, Nick hesitated, watching him walk away.

*"Cam could do with the company. Make him smile,"* Kaitlin had instructed Nick.

He wasn't sure why Cameron might be in need of anyone to make him smile. Cameron looked happy enough, still as talkative and friendly as Nick remembered him. But if Nick knew anything, it was that how people seemed on the outside didn't always match up to what they felt on the inside.

"Cam!" he called after him. "Wait up."

Cameron looked over his shoulder. His dimples

pinched his cheeks as he smiled widely and beckoned to Nick with a nod. "Come on, then."

Nick jogged forward to make up the distance between them. "So, what's with the camera?" he asked as he fell in beside him.

"It's for taking pictures with." There was a hint of sarcasm when Cameron changed the pitch of his voice in the middle of the statement.

"Funny." Nick pushed Cameron in the shoulder before cramming his hands in his pockets for warmth. "Seriously, what's it for?"

"I told you." Cameron raised the camera. "See, what happens is you point this end at the thing you want a picture of and—you see this button? If you press it—"

"I hate you," Nick interrupted. But there was no weight to his words, and he sighed.

"Okay." Cameron chuckled, then screwed up his mouth, suddenly serious. "Sorry. I figured Kaitlin would have said something about why I was taking this trip." He looked to the ground as a pained expression crossed his face.

They were at risk of straying into uncomfortable territory. With a shrug, Nick said, "She didn't really say a lot. Some work thing, was it? I don't know." He avoided mentioning the personal stuff Kaitlin had hinted was going on with him.

Cameron raised his head, more at ease when he met Nick's gaze. He stopped walking and pursed his lips thoughtfully. "Yeah. It's for a project I've been thinking of doing. I keep putting it off. Plus, I'm always so busy up in Vancouver."

"What kind of project?" Nick glanced around them. Maybe Cameron saw something he couldn't.

"A book."

Nick's instinct was to ask *what book?* But he decided against it, feeling like that child who repetitively asked why. "A book," he repeated, not feeling any less awkward for not asking his instinctive question.

"Yeah, a book." Cameron held Nick's gaze as if daring him to ask.

Nick relaxed his shoulders. *Fine.* "A book about what?"

"When I was a location scout, I'd always be on the road, meeting people, photographing possible sites for shoots. I miss it."

"I didn't know you'd stopped doing that." Nick narrowed his eyes as he tried to think back to conversations with Kaitlin where Cameron and his career might have come up.

Cameron shrugged. "I haven't given up entirely, but life got busy." He paused and appeared to be considering what to say next, as if he had to word it perfectly. "I'm an assistant location manager now, so instead of being out on the road and constantly on the move from one project to the next, I now spend more of my time prepping and being on site during filming."

Was this the personal evaluation Kaitlin had mentioned? Was Cameron, like Nick, a little lost where his career and future were concerned? Had he had second thoughts about the change in role? His loss of freedom of being on the road?

"Do you still enjoy it, even moving to be an assistant?"

Cameron glanced at him and smiled. "My job? Yeah,

of course, any way I can get it. Sure, I've had the run-in with the odd local, but it's all good."

Nick pursed his lips. *So, it's not his career, then, that he needs to sort out.* "Tell me more about this book."

When Cameron curled his lips into a gentle smile, a sense of peace and happiness lit his face. "I wanted to do something for me. I love photography. I love my job. I want to put together something that combines them. I don't know, like a locations scout's road trip, highlighting places that maybe fit different genres, maybe some sites that have been in TV shows or movies."

"Okay." Nick looked up at the buildings around the edge of the parking lot. "So, Spokane?" *What the hell is so special about Spokane that we stopped here?* The parking area looked kind of touristy, but he wasn't expecting much. Maybe a view or something, with a couple of telescopes you could look through at a dollar-fifty a pop, or even an ice-cream truck. Although at this time, with night approaching, he doubted any ice-cream vendor in their right mind would be here.

Cameron pressed his finger to his mouth, requesting silence. "Do you hear that?"

Nick listened. There was the constant but low roar he'd heard on exiting the SUV. A burst of gulls' chorus broke the spell of the soothing, almost hypnotic sound. "I guess."

"It's the falls. Thought I could get some shots, explore a little. But first—" He pulled back the sleeve of his jacket to check his watch. "—as it's almost closing time, I thought we could go ride the carousel."

"A carousel? How old are you?" Nick laughed, but felt bad when Cameron fixed his gaze on him.

There was a sense of disappointment in the way

Cameron looked at him, but also some resolve, as if he wasn't going to let Nick dissuade him from this particular adventure.

"You're never too old for a ride on a century-old carousel, Nicky."

Nick was about to protest the nickname, but Cameron was already walking away. With a huffed breath, he followed, jogging a few steps.

Cameron shortened his stride for a moment, allowing Nick to catch up. "It'll be fun."

*"Enjoy the ride and see where it takes you,"* Kaitlin had said.

Nick wasn't so sure this was the ride his sister had in mind, but still, her advice was at the forefront of his mind. Earlier at the zip line, Cameron must have wondered what the hell was wrong with him. He needed to relax; he knew that. It was just hard sometimes.

"You okay?" Cameron asked.

With a nod, Nick assured him, "I am."

*I will be.*


"HOW AWESOME WAS THAT?" Cameron was already off the carousel, hopping down the step to the concrete ground.

Nick fumbled with the leather safety strap as he unhooked it from the twisted pole. He didn't say anything at first, focusing on dismounting the black carousel horse. Swinging his leg around the back of the horse, he held onto its molded saddle and jumped down.

Cameron was looking up at him when he turned around. There was an expectant expression on his face.

"Fine. I admit it was kinda fun."

Cameron laughed. "Kinda fun. I'll take it."

Nick straightened his jacket and stepped down from beneath the bright lights of the ride.

"Have to say, I expected your aim to be better," Cameron said in a teasing tone.

The carousel had brass rings that could be collected by the occupants of the outer horses. The rings could then be tossed at a board with a painted clown, riders aiming at a hole where its mouth was.

Nick grunted, dismissing Cameron's comment. "I was a mechanic, an engineer, not a sharpshooter. What now?" It was getting late, and the early December night had sneaked up on them while they were on the carousel.

"We're losing the light," Cameron stated, looking up at the sky. "I'd like to get a few shots before we leave."

"Okay. Lead the way." Nick did the best to force the weariness from his voice.

Spokane was only an overnight stop on their road trip, so Nick couldn't argue with Cameron's desire to see whatever sights the city had to offer.

"If you want to head back to the car and wait there, I can give you the key." A fleeting look glanced over his face, something that told Nick Cameron didn't really want to go it alone.

"I'm good," Nick assured him.

Cameron's enthusiastic smile was enough to reenergize Nick, at least for a while. They followed the river, then took the trail through the falls. The sound of running water rose in volume as they got closer.

"Has much been filmed here in Spokane? Movies? TV shows?" Nick wondered aloud.

"A few things, from what I've researched." They descended a slope to the viewing area. "Johnny Depp shot a movie here."

Cameron stepped out onto the bridge and leaned against the metal railing. The low light gave the cascading water a moody feel.

Nick stood back, idly wandering to the wall that ran along the edge of the falls. He looked down at the protruding rocks and greenery. Despite the noise of rushing water, the whole experience was calming, peaceful. He breathed in deeply and watched the endless water flow. Chewing on his lip, he raised his head. Cameron stood on the bridge, lit by twilight and some man-made light.

Cameron wasn't taking photos; instead he was leaning over the railing, watching the water as Nick had done. As though he felt Nick's eyes on him, he briefly looked in Nick's direction before stepping back from the edge and moving farther along the bridge.

Something about Cameron's explanation for this trip didn't sit right with Nick. *Why are you really out here?* There was more to this trip than photographs for some book. Finding a bench, he sat and waited.

The long day was slowly beating him. Tiredness ached through every one of his limbs. Stiffly he rotated his shoulder and leaned back to look up at the sky. Clouds had blocked out any stars that might have been visible from where he was sitting. Thinning his lips, he considered their plans beyond today: almost three weeks together, with hours on the road and ten stops before home. Maybe by the end of it he would know why Cameron was really on this road trip.

Nick leaned his head back, closed his eyes, and listened to the water. A smile teased the corner of his mouth as he took the moment to relax. He hoped there would be more moments like this on their journey, time to simply stop and forget about the world. Sure, there needed to be time to think, for adventure, and for whatever else Kaitlin and Cameron had plotted between them, but peace was what he needed: pockets of time where he could remember or moments when his mind could be silent.

But all he could think about was cranberries and the fact that Christmas had taken over everywhere. He didn't really subscribe to the perfect Christmas anymore. He'd seen way too much of what was under that perfect front: families scared to own a religion, let alone focus on putting up shitty decorations. He liked the concept of the season, goodwill and all that, warmth, food and family. He just couldn't see the point of it sometimes. The commercialism, the fighting that didn't stop even for this one day a year, and the cranberries.

In fact, the season itself wasn't the only thing that fell outside his comfort zone; there was also his sister's wedding. It was only because it *was* his sister that he was even going. Add in the tackiness of a season that started way back in November, and Nick realized he would be walking around saying "Bah, humbug!" to everyone he met. He really needed to shake that thought before he arrived in Frosty Hollow.

And then there was Cameron and his talking. Nick didn't really know what to talk about in return. In the Marines, he'd talked work and with mechanics he'd talked cars. But he and Cameron had nothing in common now except for Kaitlin. The ability to form sentences that would carry a conversation had disappeared on his first tour when silence was highly valued in combat situations, interspersed with cursing and tall tales of girls they'd all slept with. Not that Nick needed to worry—most of his old squad knew him as out now, and not one of them had any issues with it, or at least no one had said anything to his face.

He pushed aside the things that made him anxious and concentrated on the noise of the falls, the coldness of the dark, and the idea that he had nothing but open road in front of him.

What seemed like a short time passed, and blinking, Nick opened his eyes. Sensing someone was watching him, he lowered his head, flinching slightly when he found Cameron resting against the wall in front of him.

"Sorry," Cameron said. "I didn't want to disturb you. You looked kind of…." He smiled. "You looked happy."

Nick could feel heat in his cheeks and hoped the lighting disguised his awkwardness. "I was just relaxing. Been a long day."

Cameron nodded. "It has. How about some food, and then we can head back to the room?"

"Did you get the photos you needed?" Nick stretched his arms out in front of him, rocking forward slightly before getting to his feet.

With a shrug, Cameron said, "It's late. I might come back in the morning. Grab a few shots of the city before we head out."

"You don't mind if I pass on that, right?" Nick questioned. He hadn't been sleeping well the last few nights and had no idea what sleep he might get tonight, having to share a room.

"I didn't expect you to accompany me. You've been dragged around enough. Think you've earned a lazy morning tomorrow." Cameron hugged his camera to his chest and lifted his shoulders as he shivered. "Might see what I have in the way of shots and end up opting for the lazy morning myself anyway. So, food?"

"Sure, why not? There were a few restaurants back the way we came."

"Excellent. Then I guess this time you can take the lead and I'll follow." He waited for Nick to make a move.

Nick met his eyes. "Okay."

*Take the lead. I can do that.*

## Chapter Four

CAMERON WOKE FIRST IN THE MORNING, STANDING AND stretching and taking a few moments to appreciate a half-naked Nick lying on top of his covers. Other than jersey boxers, he wore nothing, and seeing him splayed over the bed, all long limbs and muscles, was enough for Cameron to think that crazy staring was actually a good thing.

Nick had a Marine tattoo on his shoulder—an eagle and a globe with *USMC* in bold—and several scars marred his chest and one side. There was another tattoo Cameron couldn't get a close look at because Nick's hand lay over it, and while he had convinced himself it was okay to stare, he wasn't going to move nearer to check details. Acres of former Marine was a sight to behold, just as gorgeous as he had been all those years ago, but stronger, harder

"Staring is wrong," Nick muttered.

Cameron moved back so fast his legs caught the edge of his bed. "Just checking you were still alive."

Nick rolled up and sat on the side of his bed, his back

to Cameron. "Still breathing," he murmured. "Need coffee."

He pulled over jeans and stepped into them, and Cameron got a good look at Nick's back, unmarred by scars of any sort, and another small tattoo at the base of his neck. Dates, in a neat ordered list. He also took his fill of the sight of Nick's gorgeous ass before it was covered by denim.

But by the time Nick turned to face him, Cameron was doing a very good impression of finding socks and not looking at Nick at all.

After he'd pulled his boots on and laced them, Nick announced, "I'm going out for coffee. Back in five."

Cameron didn't answer; he nodded but didn't look up from his bag. The five minutes he'd had earlier was enough for washing himself, but he hadn't lingered. Even though he'd seen enough of Nick to get very interested, he willed away his morning wood, hoping to hell his body wouldn't rebel because while he was in the shower, he hadn't managed to get off to those perfect shoulders, the stretch of skin on Nick's back, and that tiny tattoo of dates.

Nick came back with coffee and extra cream, and then disappeared into the shower himself. Cameron thought he heard humming over the sound of the water, but couldn't swear to it.

The coffee was hot, bitter, and gave Cameron the kick-start he needed. He pulled out his small laptop and logged into his folder, uploading yesterday's photos and making sure each was properly filed and linked to the film he'd investigated, which was being shot at the falls. He added some notes about action scenes at waterfalls and researched a couple of historical photos, and Nick still hadn't emerged from the shower. The only thing that stopped him from knocking on the door and asking Nick if he was okay was the humming, which sounded distinctly like a Journey song.

He checked his email, finding two from the clinic. He clicked on them before he had a chance to even start worrying about what might be in them. One was a reminder to rearrange an assessment appointment, the other an update to his payment plan.

He closed the email page after dumping both of them in the Medical folder in his account. He kept everything they sent him, just in case.

The door to the bathroom opened and Nick walked out, with steam billowing around him as if he was walking onstage like a rock god.

A rock god in a towel. Cameron didn't know where to put his eyes, so he blurted out some shit about what they were doing today, and none of it made sense even to himself.

All Nick did was nod. Then he got dressed.

Again, Cameron looked anywhere but at the sexy guy in his room.

*I can do this. I don't have to get hard. I can look at Nick and not have flashbacks to all the orgasms I had just remembering his fucking kiss from all those years ago.*

NICK WAS PLEASED when they stopped just inside the Lolo National Forest, at a hotdog stand in a parking area. He was hungry and needed to get out of the car. After eating, they walked into the forest a short way to stretch their legs. Finally, back in the car, they reached Missoula a little after one in the afternoon.

The hotel they booked into was a Quality Inn, with views over the Clark Fork River in downtown Missoula, but it wasn't a city break that Cameron had in mind.

"Horses?" Nick stared at Cameron in disbelief. "I can't ride a horse."

"That's the point," Cameron said patiently. "There's this ranch near here that does trail rides. I booked two places, but you could just come along and watch. Or stay here." He gestured to the nondescript room.

"Stay here," Nick murmured, "or horses."

"You could always go for a walk in the city."

"Not keen on cities."

"Then come with me, and when we get there, you can sit and have a coffee. Look, they have a restaurant there, and we're booked in for dinner."

Nick glanced at the glossy brochure and wondered whether he should go through the whole folder of things that Kaitlin and Cameron had pre-organized. Just to be on the safe side.

Instead he followed Cameron down to the car, and as if sensing Nick's discomfort, Cameron handed over the keys.

"You want me to drive?" Nick asked. Cameron nodded. "Your loss if I write her off," he teased, then smiled when Cameron paled. Still, Cameron didn't make him give the keys back.

They made good time out of the city, heading south, and pulled up beside a sign for the ranch, *Crooked Tree*. Following a road over a bridge with the river below, they stopped in a large parking lot. There they got out and stretched. Cameron pointed to a small building with a sign reading Reception.

They booked in. When the guy in charge—a gorgeous cowboy with come-to-bed eyes, who said they should call him Nate—led them up a path to the stables, Nick decided he'd give this a go, after all.

Nate showed them how to tack the horses. Nick thought maybe Cameron had done this before, because he managed to get it right first time. Or was he just more observant? Seemed to Nick that Cameron was taking extra-special care to listen and learn.

And Nick himself? Well, he was kind of distracted by the sexy cowboy and how good Cameron looked in the borrowed riding boots.

"You'll be aching tomorrow if we take you too far, so as a taster, we'll walk over the river and up to a viewing place for the photos you said you wanted to get," Nate the Sexy Cowboy explained.

They mounted their horses. Cameron was a little on the slow side, but maybe Nick was faster because he still worked out and kept himself fit. Not that Cameron was unfit. Nope, he had a flat stomach with the signs of a six-pack, strong thighs, and a solid chest. But he wasn't built like a Marine like Nick.

They settled into their saddles, and another cowboy rode up, tipping his hat to Nick and Cameron. He looked kind of young to be in charge of the boisterous family that followed him in, but he, too, was built sexy. Maybe it was something in the water.

Whatever it was, Nick's eyes always strayed back to Cameron, seeing the smile on his face, the frown as they walked down a sharp incline to the wide shallow part of the river and up the other side. They rode for about fifteen minutes, and Cameron didn't take a single photo as he gripped the reins, his knuckles white.

When they stopped at the top of a hill, with the river before them, Nick listened as Nate and Cameron talked. Something about a Christmas movie filmed here earlier in the year being ready for release.

"It's been interesting," Nate said. "All the film types all over the place." He shifted forward in the saddle and pointed to the bridge where the water tumbled over the rocks beneath. "That's the best scene, the apex of the film, big fight between the hero and a cop. You probably want to get that one."

"Can you tell us what happens with the fight?" Cameron asked.

Nate shook his head. "On pain of death, no."

They laughed, exchanged more words about films and ranches and snow, and when the ride was over Nate shook their hands, asking them to send copies of the photos and maybe tag them on the ranch's new Facebook page, and even on TripAdvisor. Nick thought the cowboy was reciting that part from memory and saw him shudder as he spoke. Evidently, Nate was happier on horseback than thinking about computers.

They headed back, making their way across the water and back to the stables.

At the restaurant, they ate some kind of chicken dish with bacon, and not a cranberry in sight.

By the time they were back in Missoula, it was nine o'clock in the evening, so by mutual agreement they went up to the room. Each chose a bed.

Nick was tired, achy, and happy to lie back on the bed.

Cameron found *Terminator Genisys* on one of the channels, and they agreed to watch it. Cameron lasted about an hour, and then his breathing settled into soft, snuffly snores. He hadn't even made it under the covers or even undressed.

This wasn't a first for Nick—he'd fallen asleep in his clothes before—but the one thing he hated was when he still had shoes on, or a jacket.

Cautiously he went over to Cameron and pushed his shoulder. "Cameron?"

All Cameron did was roll over, so Nick moved to the end of the bed and unlaced his boots, easing them off and removing the socks as well. He'd never found feet sexy before, but there wasn't much about Cameron that he didn't find sexy.

*Ignore the bare feet.*

He moved to the top of the bed and began to remove Cameron's jacket, managing to push it down enough to get one arm out, but stopping when Cameron murmured something in his sleep.

It would be a good thing for Cameron to actually wake up, so Nick shook him.

Cameron opened his eyes and looked up at Nick, his expression confused, his gaze sleepy. "Hey," he muttered.

"Take your jacket off," Nick said firmly.

"Hmmm." Cameron shrugged ineffectively at the first sleeve. He looked like a turtle stuck on his back, and Nick couldn't help but smile. He leaned over to help him and let out a startled *oomph!* when Cameron gripped him and pulled him down. Sprawled over Cameron, Nick flailed for a little while but gave up as soon as Cameron yanked him hard. Abruptly they were face to face.

"Your eyes," Cameron murmured.

And then they were kissing.

Seriously, kissing.

At first it was just the press of lips, and then Cameron was pushing for entrance, demanding a deeper kiss, hands twisted in Nick's hair.

Nick didn't stand a chance. The taste of Cameron was just as he remembered, the shape of his face, the way he tugged on Nick's hair, and that Valentine's party of almost a decade ago was like it had happened yesterday.

They kissed for ages, at least it seemed that way, and Nick was caught between wanting more and knowing this was a colossally bad idea, the worst fuck-up in the history of fuck-ups.

And then the kiss stopped. Cameron released his grip, turned over onto one side, and went back to sleep.

Stunned, Nick looked down at the man who had just sent him from zero to sixty in seconds. He looked at the soft dark hair, at the way it curled a little on Cameron's forehead, at the way his lips were wet from kissing, and his ridiculously long eyelashes that were sooty black.

"What the fuck, Cameron?" Nick said. He didn't say it loud enough to wake the sleeping man, but part of him wanted to shake him awake and ask him what the hell had just happened.

Instead he went back to his bed, pulled off his clothes, and rearranged his hard cock in his boxers, maybe sliding his hand a little too slowly up his shaft and over the tip.

He even contemplated getting off right there where Cameron could roll over and watch him; the thought had him even harder.

He could do that. He could fuck his hand and make

enough noise that Cameron would wake up and maybe come over and join in.

But he didn't, of course, because that would have been a bad move.

The worst kind of move.


WHEN HE WOKE in the morning, Cameron was there with coffee. His expression was clear, as though nothing at all had happened last night.

"Ready in ten. We have to get to Billings, but there are stops along the way. Thought we'd take it easy. The next thing isn't booked until the fourth."

Nick showered and dressed, and all that time he waited for Cameron to mention the kiss.

But no—he didn't say a goddamned thing.

And there was no way in hell Nick was saying anything. He should keep his mouth shut and chalk it up to a weird, kissing, dream-type sequence that Cameron had going on in his head.

Yep, definitely best that way.

# Chapter Five

ALL CAMERON COULD THINK WAS THAT IT HAD BEEN A dream. He had to have imagined the delicious, sexy sensation of Nick's lips on his. Right?

The drive to Billings had been odd, like there had been this tension between them that Cameron couldn't explain. Maybe it had been his imagination, but the more he had thought about it, the more he'd wanted to ask Nick straight out what his problem was.

The kiss. No way did that happen for real.

*But what if it had?*

Cameron pushed in his earbuds and scrolled through the playlists on his phone. He selected a mix of dance tunes, then turned up the volume when the beat kicked in. They had checked in to the hotel a couple of hours ago and made some unspoken agreement to do their own thing.

Stretching his neck from side to side, Cameron eyed the street ahead as he waited for the GPS on his watch to pinpoint his position. After deciding a run would be the best way to clear his head, he'd done a quick search of the area and plotted himself a route. He set his watch, took a few steps, and was barely setting a pace before the volume dipped and his phone rang. Grumbling, he slowed to a walk and pulled his phone from his waistband so he could see who was calling.

*Kaitlin. Great.*

He swiped the screen, accepting the call.

"Not interrupting anything, am I?" Kaitlin asked in a less than subtle tone.

Lowering the call volume a little, he spoke into the mic on his earbuds. "No. Nothing."

"You okay?"

"Of course. Why?" He knew he had answered too quickly and too faux cheerfully.

"What's happened? Is Nick being a dick and not joining in?"

The urge to defend Nick rolled over in his stomach. "What? No. He's been fine."

Kaitlin went quiet. She was clearly trying to figure out if something was wrong.

To reassure her, he said again, "Everything is fine. Seriously. It's only been three days. What could possibly have happened?"

He imagined her narrowing her eyes, pursing her lips, looking him in the eye, and refusing to look away until he cracked. So of course, he did. "Have you ever had a moment where you're not sure if something really happened or if it was a dream?"

"What kind of something?" There was suspicion in her voice.

"I don't know. How about held a conversation with someone?" Cameron walked a few feet. He turned around and looked back along the street. He could make out the roof of the hotel over the top of some trees.

Kaitlin said something he didn't catch, but he realized she was talking to someone at her end. "Sorry about that," she said. "Jamie wanted to know if I wanted takeout tonight. I never seem to remember dreams all that well, so not sure I can help you with that. I've woken up mid-conversation with Jamie in the past. Not a clue what I've been talking about." She laughed.

"Sleep-talking," Cameron uttered. Was sleep-kissing a thing?

"Yeah. Think I reeled off the weekly shopping list one night."

Cameron chuckled. "How romantic."

"Mmm. Anyway, how are things going? Not seen many updates. Not that I'm stalking your social media or anything. Far too much to do juggling the wedding and my mother."

The formidable Mrs. Sheridan could be quite the handful at times, mostly rooted in her desire for perfection.

"Your mom still thinks she knows what's best, I take it?"

"On every day that ends in *y*."

"I told you moving to the opposite side of the country to my folks had its perks. At least I get away from talking about the ex face to face."

He fell silent, taking a moment to reflect on his words. Sure, he didn't have his mother on his case every five minutes, but it had also isolated him from too many people who might have cared about the shitty mess he'd gotten himself into with Travis. The memory of pain shooting up his back as Travis had pushed him back against his apartment wall caused him to wince. That had been the first and last time his boyfriend got physical with him. Cameron just wished he had gotten out sooner, avoided all the arguments and verbal battering.

*Life's too short.*

Kaitlin pulled him from his thoughts. "Hey, you're not thinking about *Travis*, are you?"

"What? No." Cameron swallowed hard. "Not really." He pulled at the sleeve of his sports T-shirt. "Nick's doing okay, by the way."

"Smooth with the change of subject." She snorted a soft laugh. "I'll go with it. So, did he actually get on a horse?"

Cameron breathed in deeply, grateful she didn't pursue the subject of Travis. The man was an ass, and Cameron had wasted too much time on him already. "He did."

"Did you take a photo?"

"I think he might have gotten in a shot or two."

"And these aren't on Facebook because…?" She quickly added, "Were there any hot cowboys?"

Cameron laughed. "One or two." His mood brightened. "Anything else you'd like to know, or can I carry on with my run?"

"Okay, I'll take the hint. I just wanted to check in on my best friend and make sure my brother hadn't driven him to murder yet. I would like you both in one piece when you get here."

Murder hadn't crossed Cameron's mind. Not yet,

anyway. It had only been three days. "I promise, no murdering."

"Right, I guess I'll let you get back to your run." She paused.

*Please don't ask about the assessment.*

Kaitlin was his best friend, and good or bad, they told each other everything. Had done since the days of building forts out of dining chairs and sheets, cuddling up together among a pile of pillows and blankets to whisper their secrets. He blinked, trying not to lose the whimsical memories for ones of sterile hospital wards and sympathetic faces.

*I can't do that again.*

He relaxed when she said, "Say hi to Nick for me. I'll catch up with him in a couple of days."

"Sure. Bye for now."

"Bye." Kaitlin hung up.

The dance track faded back in and he closed his eyes, listening to the bass beat as it resonated through him. Then, opening his eyes, he rotated his shoulders, shrugged off the grim memories and his fears for the future, reset his watch, and focused on the sidewalk ahead of him.

It was going to be a long three weeks.

THE RUN WAS enough to clear his head, and he stretched out before going back into the hotel and exchanging pleasantries with the staff who had gathered in the outside smoking area.

The irony of walking through the smoking area to get into a smoke-free hotel never failed to amuse him, but he held his breath the entire time he walked through the fog.

No sense in taking risks, even if the jury was out on whether second-hand smoke in such small amounts meant anything at all.

Nick had said he was going out to explore, and he wasn't back by the time Cameron got to the room, so he took the time to lock the bathroom door, shave, and then shower, all at his own pace.

Kaitlin had said she talked in her sleep, so he shouldn't be so hard on himself. The kiss was a dream. It had to be, because he'd spent so many years recalling the real kiss that he'd convinced himself he would never be able to kiss Nick again.

There was no way he would have yanked Nick down on him, held him so he couldn't tug away, and then forced a kiss on him.

Embarrassment flooded him and he sat heavily on the side of the bath; the water in the shower was still falling and filling the bathroom with steam. Why couldn't he just do things properly and not have to sit afterward and negotiate his way through the minefield that was his thoughts?

*Why did I stay with Travis?*

*Why did I let Travis hurt me? What kind of man does that?*

*And why am I so set on avoiding the hospital every time they ring?*

He clambered into the shower and washed his hair over and over, thankful for the unending supply of hot water, and he settled his embarrassment, the questions, and the whole of his life to a single point, focusing on the next minute, the next hour, the next day.

*Always look forward.*

He wrapped a towel around his waist and decided that tonight he wanted a drink.

A beer. Whisky. Vodka. He didn't care what, just needed the burn of it.

He had to get Nick to agree to go with him. Because there was no way in hell he was going to be the sad, pathetic idiot who drank alone in a corner.

## Chapter Six

NICK LEFT THE ELEVATOR AND STOPPED TO RECALL WHICH way led to their room. He didn't very often use elevators, preferring to take the stairs as much as he could. But, stupidly worse the wear for the beers he'd drunk, he'd chosen the elevator, randomly pressing buttons until finally the doors opened on the third floor.

He walked to the stair exit and then turned with his back to the door, getting his bearings. Was it 329 or 392? When it became obvious there was no 392, he followed the sign that included 329, and as stealthily as he could, let himself in. He could hear the shower and so sat on his bed, waiting for Cameron to come out.

The door opened and Cameron exited, clearly in a world of his own, without spotting Nick.

"Hey," Nick said.

Cameron jumped at the greeting and pressed a hand to his heart. "Jesus Christ!"

It was all Nick could do not to fixate on the fact

Cameron was only wearing a towel. "Sorry. Didn't mean to scare you."

"I didn't hear you come in." Cameron tightened the towel around his waist. His hair was wet and slicked back, and droplets of water clung to his skin, catching the light in shimmering streaks.

"Sorry," Nick said again. Mesmerized by the tiny glints of light on Cameron's body, his eyes flicked all over his damp form. "How was your run?"

His gaze settled on Cameron's chest. He got an up-close-and-personal look at the tattoo on his chest: it looked like a ship in a bottle, beached and framed in roses. Interesting choice… Nick wondered what it meant.

Nick's Marine Corps tattoo was for friendship and loyalty and for his team, built on adversity. The rose on his side for his sister, thorns and all. And the dates on his back were important to him—vital—marking events he would likely never talk about to another person.

He opened his mouth to ask about Cameron's, but knowing his own need for privacy, he decided against it and shut it again.

Cameron grabbed a T-shirt off his bed and pulled it on, swiftly covering the beautiful design. The water that had lingered on his shoulders and chest now darkened the gray material in damp spots. "It was good. Thanks."

He rolled the T-shirt down to meet his towel, then turned his back as he attempted to pull his boxers on with the towel in place. With his small jump, it fell away. After the briefest flash of the top of Cameron's buttocks, his underwear was up.

Leaning back, Nick admired the view as Cameron bent down to collect his towel from the floor. He thought back to the night before, to sleepy Cameron and the kiss. Part of him wanted to ask what it was all about, but he didn't want to embarrass him. Cameron and he were getting on okay, and they still had a long way to go before they got back to Frosty Hollow. Best not rock the boat.

*You could always jump ship and get a flight.*

Cameron glanced over his shoulder; Nick lifted his gaze, aware he'd been caught looking.

An awkward silence fell between them.

Just as Nick was going to apologize, Cameron jumped in to save the day.

"What did you get up to when you were out?" he asked.

Nick shrugged. "Not so much. Explored a bit. Found a bar. Pulled up a stool." He smiled brightly at Cameron. Those beers had relaxed him.

"A bar." Cameron hung up his towel. "Kaitlin called. She was asking after you."

Nick blew out a breath and lay down on the bed. He pulled his jacket closed around him. "Checking I'm not wrecking the trip, I assume?"

Cameron moved to stand by the bed, then looked down at him. "She just wanted to know you were okay. Which you are, right?" He held Nick's gaze.

"Yep."

Cameron narrowed his eyes for a moment but seemed to decide against pressing it further.

Nick sighed, sitting back up. "Honestly. It's all good."

"That's what I told her." Cameron finished getting dressed.

Pursing his lips, Nick eyed the far wall. He had thought some time to himself might have kick-started the whole thinking thing he'd promised Kaitlin he would do on this trip. Instead he'd just felt more confused and had opted to ignore it for a while longer. A bar and a beer had seemed as good a distraction as any.

"Did you want to do anything else tonight?" Cameron sat on his bed, sitting cross-legged on the mattress.

Nick had no idea what was in the plan for tomorrow, but he liked the idea of something simple. "How about you join me for a drink? We could go back to the bar I found— it's only a few minutes away, shoot some pool, eat some bar snacks."

"How many beers have you had already?" Cameron raised an eyebrow.

Nick frowned. One or two, maybe three. It was definitely more than one, and not that crappy light beer, but the real stuff. "Just a couple," he hedged.

Cameron shook his head, a quiet affection on his face. "Maybe we should get you something to eat first."

Considering the soft focus he was currently viewing Cameron in, food sounded a sensible idea. With a slow nod, he agreed. "Okay." He smiled at Cameron, who smiled back, and a warmth ached deep in Nick's chest.

Cameron uncrossed his legs. "I'll get my coat."

Which was how they ended up at Murphy's Irish Pub, in the middle of nowhere, shooting pool with a group of bikers, one of whom was called Killer and was ex-Navy. And how they both managed to drink way too much than was good for them.

Somehow, they made it back to the room, holding each other up, laughing at everything and nothing.

Nick hadn't felt this free and uninhibited in a very long

time. He laughed as he dropped onto the bed, dragging Cameron with him.

They lay next to each other.

With a heavy sigh, Nick rolled onto his back and stared up at the ceiling. "I'm going to regret this in the morning, aren't I?" He hadn't intended to drink so much, but he'd been having a good time. It was easy to relax, talk, and laugh with a beer in his hand. "Neither of us is driving tomorrow," he added, carefully sounding out each word.

Freeing himself from Nick's hold, Cameron straightened up. "For a big burly Marine, you're kind of a lightweight." He kicked off his shoes, then looked down at Nick with a smile in his eyes. "I told you to quit while you were ahead."

"I owed Killer a beer for winning the game," Nick pointed out, because that made a lot of sense. "But I know," he grumbled and rested his arm over his face, already imagining the hangover. "Please tell me you plan to be gentle with me tomorrow. No more horses and zip lines." He stretched his hands above his head, curling his fingers in the bedding.

"I promise." Cameron pursed his lips, his gaze lingering for a moment.

"Take a picture," Nick said.

"What?" Cameron blinked and turned away.

Nick rolled onto his side and watched him. "That's what they say, isn't it? Take a picture, it'll last longer."

Cameron glanced back over his shoulder. "Ah." He kept his back to Nick as he unbuttoned his shirt.

With a grunt, Nick sat up. Tiredly, he pulled at the zipper of his jacket and shrugged the material from his shoulder. He cast a sideways glance at Cameron as they finished undressing in silence. "No goodnight kiss tonight?" he said, shuffling up the bed. He knew it was a bad move the minute he said it, but seemed alcohol made him think he was funny.

Cameron pulled back his sheet. "Kiss?" He looked panicked as he slid under the covers.

"You kissed me," Nick said. Cameron seemed to shrug the comment off and turned out the lamp at his side of the room. "So… you were asleep. Huh. I've heard of sleepwalking and talking, but *kissing*—"

"Crap" was all Cameron said.

"Apparently, you like my eyes," Nick continued. "Do you like my eyes?" He stared at Cameron.

Cameron opened his mouth but didn't say anything.

Nick really should take Cameron's advice and quit while he was ahead, but the beer had made him reckless. "I like your eyes." With a smirk, he shuffled beneath the comforter. "Sorry, I didn't mean to tease." He turned out his own light. "It was a bit confusing." He stared up at the dark ceiling.

"I really did that?"

"You really did."

"I'm so sorry."

Nick turned his head. "Don't worry about it." He could just make out Cameron in the dark. "I didn't mind."

"Good night, Nick." Cameron rolled over.

*I am such an idiot.* Nick returned his attention to the ceiling, focusing on the low glow from the moving lights of a passing car. *Why did I have to bring it up?* He closed his eyes, rolled over, and hugged his pillow. He could remember the kiss so clearly: the feel of Cameron's mouth pressed firmly to his.

*Really, I didn't mind at all.*

# Chapter Seven

*Kill me now.*

Cameron folded his arms across his chest and watched the information video. He was about to be thrown into Wonderland with Nick, and it was down to them to find their way out by solving a string of puzzles.

*Wonderland. I'm going to* kill *Kaitlin.*

Cameron didn't need reminding of the first time he made a complete idiot of himself where kissing Nick was concerned. It had been his first kiss with a guy. Actually, his first kiss with anyone.

A young woman stepped forward as the video hit the end. She was surprisingly tall, dressed in a black T-shirt with the company logo emblazoned on it, and had the hair of an anime character, bright blue with heavy bangs and tied up in bunches either side of her head. "Okay. You have sixty minutes to escape the room." She spoke with her hands. "Anything and everything could be a clue except the countdown screen. So, no touching that." She waggled a finger at them. "So, are we ready?"

Cameron glanced at Nick. "Ready?"

"As I'll ever be." In a lower voice, he added, "I don't see this helping my headache."

So, Nick's hangover had finally kicked in.

"Just be glad there aren't any horses." Cameron pushed his hands in the front pockets of his jeans and gave anime girl an enthusiastic nod.

"This way, gentlemen." She led them along a narrow corridor and stopped outside the door. "The clock starts when I shut the door." She held the door open for them.

Nick took the lead, giving a small grumble as he stepped inside. "Dear God."

Cameron followed him inside and stopped abruptly. He couldn't help but laugh at the decorated room. There were large plastic mushrooms, a table with a tea set, plated fake slices of cakes, and cards. Lots and lots of playing cards.

Nick glanced around the room. "I feel like I'm back at Kaitlin's Valentine's party." As the door clicked shut, Cameron looked over his shoulder. Kaitlin had booked the experience. "I think she did this on purpose." She knew about the kiss in senior year and the crush he'd had on Nick as a teenager.

Nick said, "It's like some horrific flashback."

*Horrific*? Had the party really been that bad in Nick's mind? Cameron glanced around the room. This was going to be an uncomfortable hour.

Nick examined the door. "Need a code to get out. Buttons are numbered zero to five."

The clock was already ticking down on the television screen. On the table a variety of objects stood between the plastic props. "*Play me*," Cameron read and picked up a small glass jar, the catch on the lid fastened with a padlock. Inside was a flash drive.

"I'm guessing we don't just smash the jar and get it out," Nick said

"No," Cameron said. "That would be too easy. Can you see a laptop or something lying around?" He turned the jar over. "Or a key?" He glanced at Nick, who was standing in the corner of the room. "Nick?"

"Need another two keys over here."

Cameron looked around Nick to see a sign. "Escape is down the rabbit hole."

"There's something in there. Maybe it's the code we need." Nick crouched down and tugged at something.

Curious, Cameron stood behind Nick and looked down to where the sign was pointing. Sunk into the floor was a circular container large enough for a grown man to fit his hand inside. Two padlocks secured a plastic lid that was semi-transparent, a bubble-like pattern obscuring the view of whatever was inside.

Nick ran his fingers around the edge of the container's cover. "We're not getting in there until we get the locks off."

Huffing a breath, Cameron looked around the room; there was some writing on one the mushrooms. "One equals spades."

"What?"

"Two equals hearts."

Nick came to stand beside him. "Three is clubs and four diamonds." He quirked an eyebrow. "And?"

"And… I have no idea. A code, maybe." He turned back to the table. "Okay, where do we start?"

Nick examined the table and picked up a wooden box. Shaking it, he frowned at the sound of something rattling inside. He met Cameron's eyes expectantly and held out the box.

"Don't look at me. You're the mechanic." Cameron left him to fight with box while he continued to explore the room. Ducking down, he checked underneath the table and each of the chairs. Under each chair was one of the suits from a pack of cards. Each chair was a different color. Back on his feet, he crossed to the other side of the room, where a locked cupboard with another padlock required four letters to open it. He rotated the cylinders, examining the letters. Should they spell a word?

"Ah-ha!" Nick exclaimed behind him.

"Did you do it?"

The puzzle box was not open, but Nick had managed release one of the blocks. "Not so much." He tossed the freed piece onto the table and rotated the box, then raised his head. "Is this some kind of revenge? Did I do something to upset Kaitlin?" He laughed, pushing and pulling at the blocks that made up the box.

"She just wants you to have some fun," Cameron said without thinking.

"You two been talking about me?"

There was a strained expression on Nick's face as he focused on the box. Was he pissed?

He could understand why Nick might be annoyed. "Only as much as I'm sure you two have talked about me." He cast Nick a sideways glance and studied his face for any clues as to exactly what Kaitlin might have told him.

The tension was brief, then Nick said, "I can think of more fun things to do than allowing myself to be locked in a room for an hour." He tapped the edge of the wooden box against the palm of his hand.

Cameron glanced at the clock. They were already down five minutes. "Okay. You get us out of this room and we'll do that."

"Do what?"

*I can't believe I'm going to say this.* "You can pick what we do for the next couple of stops."

"Go off plan? Now, let's not be too rash." Nick laughed.

"I'm serious." Cameron held out his hand. "Deal?"

"Okay, deal. But you join in. No matter what I pick."

"Sure."

Nick gave Cameron's hand a sharp shake, then, with a triumphant sound, thrust the box in Cameron's direction. "Admit it. You're a little bit impressed." He tipped the box up and a key fell out into his hand; then he swapped the box for the Play Me jar with the flash drive and tried the key in the padlock, disappointed when the key didn't turn. "Wrong key."

Cameron cocked his head. "Or wrong lock." He nodded to the rabbit hole.

Crouching down, Nick tried the key again. "Okay. One down." He held the open padlock above his head. "Now we just need to find the other key."

Cameron cast his gaze around the room. Maybe this wasn't really the kind of fun either of them needed.

THE HOUR WAS ALMOST UP. Through a series of tasks, Nick and Cameron had managed to find various keys and codes to further their escape. Along the way, they had revealed a small laptop, unlocked the Play Me jar, and watched the flash drive.

Cameron glanced over to where Nick was still musing over the answer to the series of questions they had found on the flash drive. It had given them a time but they had no idea what it was for yet.

Cameron pulled the drawer out of the dresser and turned it over, surprised to find a flashlight taped to the underside.

Peeling back the tape, he freed the flashlight. He shook the flashlight gently not sure what he was expecting. It was just a light. He turned it on, pursing his lips as he eyed the colored glow. "It's a UV flashlight." Cameron shone the light on the back of his hand. "Can we turn out the lights in here?" He clicked the flashlight off and on a couple of times, shining it over various objects near to him. They had seven minutes left on the clock.

"I think so." Nick crossed the room. "Yeah, there's a switch." He turned off the lights.

The room plunged into darkness. Cameron turned the flashlight on and slowly moved it around the room.

"Stop," Nick said. "The wall."

Cameron moved closer. A word was scrawled across the wall, revealing itself as the UV light hit it. "*Overdue*," he read. He moved the light a little further to where another word glowed.

"*Slow*," Nick said. He was standing close to Cameron. "How many letters did the padlock on the cupboard need?"

"Four," Cameron remembered. "Try *slow*—that's four letters." He blinked as Nick switched the lights back on.

Nick checked the cupboard lock. "There's no *s*."

Cameron shone the flashlight up on the ceiling. "Wait. I think there's more."

A further spell of darkness revealed two more words. *After*. *Tardy*.

"Four words. Maybe we need to take the first letter of each," Cameron mused.

"Overdue, after, slow, tardy. What do they all imply?" Nick's voice rose at the end; it was apparent he already knew the answer, which he gave with a grin. "*Late*, right? Like the rabbit in the story."

"Not just a pretty face," Cameron teased.

It didn't take Nick long to rotate the cylinders on the padlock to spell *late*. He smiled when he was successful, and after removing the lock, he opened the cupboard.

"Please tell me we're nearly done." Cameron frowned when Nick pulled out a circular box with four colored buttons on the top.

Nick checked the underside of the box. He rested it on the table and pressed one of the buttons. Nothing happened. He tried each in turn. The third button he pressed made a clicking sound and remained depressed. Nick tried the lid again, twisting and pulling, but to no avail. He hit another button, huffing a breath as the depressed button popped back up.

"Colors. The chairs." He looked around the table. "Blue, green, yellow, red."

"Same as the buttons."

Cameron glanced at the clock. Four minutes—where had the time gone? "Okay so they had the playing card suits on the bottom of them and… the code. Maybe it's the order." He turned each of the chairs over. "So, one equals spades and the spade is on the yellow chair. Is that what you pressed before?"

Nick pressed the yellow button, third in line, nodding as it stayed down. "What did two equal?"

"Hearts, and that's on the red chair," Cameron said.

Nick pressed the red button, smiling when it too stayed down.

"Which leaves blue, then green."

Each button stayed down and finally Nick was able to pull the lid off. "The other key!" Quickly he was on the other side of the room, down by the rabbit hole, releasing the second padlock. "It's a pocket watch." He handed it over to Cameron.

The watch was gold with a long chain hanging from it. The time was set to one thirty. "One thirty. What was the other one? The time we worked out?"

"Two forty-five."

Cameron repeated the times over in his head, and at almost the same moment, he and Nick said, "Two, four, five, one, three, zero!"

It had to be the code for the door.

Before Cameron even had a chance to think about moving, Nick was there, typing in the digits. With each button, a small green light lit above the number. The code was correct and the lock clicked as it seemed to release.

"Together?" Nick held his hand over the handle and waited for Cameron to join him.

Cameron wrapped his hand around Nick's and they pressed down together; the handle moved and the door swung open. In the confusion of victory and excitement, they hugged. The feel of Nick in his arms was almost overwhelming. Nick, warm and solid, brought back memories of what had been missing the last couple of months. Cameron had gotten used to sharing his life with someone, no matter how unhealthy that relationship had been, and he'd found the adjustment to single life harder than he'd expected, especially now. Maybe he did need someone, their support and love to get him through the bad days.

He felt a little dizzy and didn't know whether that was because he was in Nick's arms or the shadow of illness that hung over him.

Realizing the hug was going on a little too long, he pulled back and looked at the clock. "Just over a minute to spare."

Anime Girl was waiting for them outside. "Well done, gentlemen, on beating the room." She handed them signs expressing their success at escaping and asked them to pose for a photograph.

Cameron smiled brightly, surprised when Nick put his arm around him and hugged him close for the picture.

They exited through the gift shop and made their way outside.

"I was wrong," Nick said.

Cameron slowed his pace and they stopped when they were out on the sidewalk. "About what?"

"Don't tell Kaitlin, but that was pretty fun, if I'm honest."

Cameron laughed. "Yeah, I guess it was."

"But we did escape, and you made a deal." Nick looked pleased with himself.

"Yes, I did." He studied Nick curiously. There was mischief in his eyes. "Am I going to regret it?"

Nick simply smiled, turned on his heel, and started walking in the direction of the car.

Cameron followed. "You're so mean."

"Just you wait."

Heat sparked in Cameron's chest as Nick widened his smile and directed it at him. Apprehension and excitement fused within him. Part of him was really looking forward to the next couple of days.

*I can't wait.*

## Chapter Eight

Nick woke from an intense dream that had him rolling straight out of bed and onto his feet in a crouch, his heart pounding, and his skin damp with sweat. He couldn't remember the dream but whatever it was left a residue of adrenaline that made him shaky.

"You okay?" Cameron asked sleepily.

"Yeah." Nick didn't elaborate, disappearing into the bathroom and cursing under his breath. Waking up like that hadn't happened in a long time; he really thought he'd got all the crap in his head under control.

*Guess not.*

"I'm getting coffee!" Cameron called through the bathroom door.

"Okay," Nick answered and then went back to staring at himself in the mirror.

Last night they'd watched a rerun of an old *Friends* episode and fallen asleep with the lights on. When Nick did his usual middle-of-the-night wake-up, a habit he hadn't broken since his time overseas, he had turned everything off.

This morning he wasn't tired; he just felt odd, like a buzzing under his skin and he couldn't identify what it was.

He showered, then dressed, all before Cameron came back with the coffee, and by the time he was sipping the black stuff, he was feeling way more in control of himself.

Cameron sat on the side of his bed. "Happens sometimes?" he asked.

"What?"

"Nightmares."

"Some."

Cameron nodded. "I'm sorry you have those."

"It is what it is," Nick dismissed. "So, what do you think for today? Army assault course? Triathlon?" He smiled when Cameron blanched at the words. "I'm joking with you, we need to get to our next hotel. Where is it, by the way?"

He'd never seen anyone look so relieved as Cameron at that point.

"Rapid City, five hours."

"And what did Kaitlin have organized for us, so I know if we need to work round it?"

Cameron pulled over the notebook and checked. "It's just a driving day. There are some things tomorrow morning."

"Okay, then. Today we get to Rapid City, and I have plans."

"You do?"

"Well, I have ideas," Nick admitted.

"Like what?"

"That would be telling."

He started packing up, Cameron did the same, and they were on the road after breakfast. The journey was uneventful, hours listening to a radio that would cut out whenever they passed through town limits, switching to the next station, and commenting on the eighties music that seemed to rule the playlists of all of the local stations.

They reached Rapid City by early afternoon. They shared the driving and talked about the landscape, (mostly unchanging), the weather, (the same), and the chances of the Seahawks reaching the Superbowl. And in between, Nick racked his brains as to what they could do when they reached Rapid City. He still felt tense, even though he was trying really hard to relax, and he put part of the blame for that on Cameron.

Cameron, who kept glancing at him as they drove, seeming to have something on his mind. In fact, Nick was waiting for him to get all serious and start talking about the kiss again—or worse, Nick's feelings or something equally uncomfortable.

The Grand Gateway Hotel was pretty nice; a step up from a Holiday Inn, at least. The beds were firm, the room large, and the hotel had a pool. Nick hadn't gone swimming in a while now, and he resolved to buy some trunks so he could go. Cameron agreed, and they stopped at a sports store on their way to the one thing that Nick *really* wanted to do.

They were here. And Cameron wasn't happy, if the squawk of outrage was anything to go by.

He finally managed to say "I am not, I repeat *not*, getting up on a stage and singing."

Nick simply pressed a hand to the small of Cameron's back and guided him in. "Yes, you are. That was the deal."

"Nick—"

"And this place does the best chiliburgers."

"But—"

"You know you like to live dangerously."

"I can't sing," Cameron moaned as they crossed the threshold into the bar and sat at a table to one side. There were small groups of people, drinking, chatting, eating, but Cameron's wide-eyed gaze was fixed firmly on the small stage and the karaoke set up.

"What can I get you?" a server asked.

"Beer, whatever's on tap," Nick told her. "Cameron?"

Cameron turned to face him, his eyes wide, and then glanced back at the small stage with the microphone stand. "Vodka. Triple."

The server exchanged a look with Nick that spoke of understanding, and she left them with the menu.

Nick really tried to concentrate on his, but he couldn't take his eyes off Cameron and the scared expression on his face. "I'll go first," he reassured him. "It doesn't start for an hour or so." He closed the menu, already knowing what he was going to order.

"Why would you go up alone?" Cameron asked suspiciously. "I thought we were doing this together?"

The bar was filling up. The server took their orders—both chose the trademark chiliburgers—and Cameron was still waiting for an answer.

"I get you're nervous, but this is no worse than some of the idiot things you and Kaitlin post on Facebook."

"I would rather rappel down the Empire State Building than sing in a bar." Cameron shuddered.

Nick considered there were two ways to play this: he could call Cameron on the deal and demand that he went up there, or he could use some passive aggression that he'd learned from Kaitlin. "You don't have to. I'll just do my turn after we eat, is all."

"Really?" Cameron seemed to relax a little, but there was still some suspicion in his expression.

"Yep. No one here will think any less of you, least of all me."

Their food arrived, and in no particular order, several people went up on stage and crucified various songs. It didn't matter, though. Everyone was in groups, happy and laughing, and no one called anyone on their abilities. Cameron even seemed to unwind more as the evening went on, and that was a good thing for both of them to relax.

"My turn," Nick said and made his way through the tables to the stage, selecting a song and then taking up his position.

The music was all Christmas-themed, and he knew exactly which song he wanted to sing right then.

He got a few wolf whistles, some cheers, and then the opening bars of "Thank God It's Christmas" filled the room. He channeled his inner Freddie Mercury and everyone started to sing along. This was *the* karaoke song for him at Christmas, and he didn't even have to follow the words. The mic expanded his voice over the top of everyone else, and as he sang, he remembered other times when the sheer happiness of singing had made every other worry vanish.

He couldn't see Cameron because the small spotlight was enough to blind him, but he liked to think that he was singing okay and maybe he could get Cameron up onstage. When his song finished, a round of applause rang out and he sketched a small bow, knocked sideways when Cameron jumped up next to him.

"Let's do this," Cameron shouted over the clapping, still wide-eyed and likely crapping himself, but he'd joined Nick on the stage, and that was freaking awesome.

"What are you doing up here?"

"Don't leave me. Tell me what we're singing."

"You know 'Baby It's Cold Outside'?"

"Yeah."

Cameron nodded at the skinny guy at the controls and leaned in with the request.

And then magic happened.

Off-key, shouty magic, but enough that they left the stage, grinning madly with their arms around each other like two drunken idiots. They'd even done another song, changing the words to "I'm Gonna Be (500 miles)" to "*I would* drive *five hundred miles*" and laughing at their own jokes even as they tried to sing.

They didn't move from the bar all night. Nick went up once more on his own, and Cameron got up to go on his own but chickened out at the last moment, demanding Nick go with him.

When they left the bar, Nick's ears were buzzing and he felt spaced out and kind of high.

They were only a few steps from the bar when Cameron grabbed his arm, dragging him into the shadows in the alley and pushing him against the wall.

"Do you know how fucking hot that was?" Cameron husked. It clearly wasn't a question. "You up there singing and grinning and gyrating, and all I wanted to do was kiss you right there."

Nick curled his hand around Cameron's face, cradling him. This could either be amazing or go really badly, very quickly. "How much did you drink?" he asked cautiously.

"A beer, one vodka," Cameron said, quickly adding, "It's not the drink."

"Cameron."

"No, Nick, this is stupid. I want to kiss a man, I should be able to kiss him, right? If he wants to, I mean." He said the last bit with a wry smile.

"Yes, of course."

"And I want to kiss you."

"Okay."

"Really? Okay?"

Nick shrugged. He wasn't the wordy one here; Cameron was in control of this. The kiss they shared years ago didn't go so well, and he'd half expected that Cameron would kiss him and then shove him away like last time. He hadn't then, why would he do it now?

Their gazes met and held, and at that point Nick could move away and laugh this off as beer and fun, nothing more. But he couldn't. He'd already tasted Cameron once, so many years ago, then again the other night, and all he wanted was one more taste, however stupid they were being.

Cameron appeared to have no such concerns, and he crowded into Nick's space. Abruptly the sound from the bar, the voices of people nearby, and the cold and ice of a snowy December night all vanished. Then it was just the taste of Cameron and the way he stole Nick's breath.

Nick linked his hands behind Cameron's head, holding

him still, and there was no way they could feel each other in their bulky parkas but, jeez, it was so hot.

Until the cold seeped in.

"The hotel is five minutes' walk," Cameron whispered.

Nick had a decision to make. He could do something incredibly clever and chalk this up to the romance of the karaoke, if you could call it that. Or he could accept that this thing between them had been building for a long time and might even have happened if Nick hadn't signed up.

"It's okay, you know," Cameron whispered, his breath puffs of white in the dark. "We don't have to do anything."

And that was it, his out. All he had to do was say that they'd had fun, but his sister was Cameron's best friend, and so it would be a hundred kinds of uncomfortable.

But all he did was hold out his hand and wait to see what Cameron did.

And Cameron? He curled his gloved hand into Nick's, and together they walked to the hotel.

## Chapter Nine

THEY DIDN'T TALK AS THEY WALKED, NOR AS THEY WAITED for the elevator, nor even as Nick took the initiative and opened the hotel room door.

Only when they were inside did everything change.

Cameron slipped off his jacket and scarf and put it on the back of the chair, waiting for something from Nick. Anything. Because right at that moment, Cameron had gone from aggressive need to feeling stupid and shy. He'd gotten up onstage, risen to the comment about how no one would judge him when Nick knew damn well *everyone* would look at the one guy who wouldn't sing. Cameron wasn't that man; he was the one who took chances in the life he'd been gifted.

So, he'd sung with Nick, and it had been wonderful, and liberating, and fun. And then they'd kissed outside.

Nick interrupted Cameron's thoughts by moving to stand right in front of him as soon as he'd shed his coat. "So, we're finally doing this?" he asked.

Cameron reached out and cradled Nick's face. Nick's

skin was cold from the outside, his lips still parted after the question.

Alcohol was loosening Cameron's tongue, and he had so much he wanted to say that he wouldn't even think of saying usually.

"Do you know how much I wanted you before?" he asked, with no regrets. "You were so fucking gorgeous, wearing these worn jeans that fitted you everywhere. And so sexy. God, so sexy."

Nick chuckled, but it wasn't a sound filled with derision, but rather as if he found Cameron's words cute. Then he blew Cameron's worries out of the water. "Probably as much as I wanted the sexy guy who was coming onto me."

Cameron could remember that night; dressed as one of the many Mad Hatters, he'd worn a hat to hide his ubershort hair.

"Sexy? Yeah, right. My hair was still growing back, and I was so skinny. You don't have to make it sound better than it was."

Great, bring thoughts of the Big C into an intimate encounter. *Way to go, Cameron.*

"Your hair was cute, and so soft, and you fit perfectly in my arms," Nick murmured. "Is it okay to say that about your hair?"

And there it was: cancer, front and center.

"It was a long time ago. The cancer, I mean. It's fine to talk about it."

And yes, he was lying. Cancer was a specter that loomed over him every fucking day. From the dizziness, to the weakness, and shortness of breath, he knew that something was crawling inside him; he just knew.

Nick smiled and clearly didn't see the lie Cameron had just told. "Then I can say that at the party you looked good, well, happy, and excited. And you wanted to kiss me and I wanted to kiss you."

Cameron couldn't help but return the smile. "You were everything I wanted then. All my fantasies and my hopes rolled into one." He stopped. Was it stupid to admit things like that? Feelings so deep that he'd lost the sense of them even being there. "But honestly, you don't have to pretend, I know you just wanted to make me feel good."

"What do you mean?"

"You don't have to say you wanted to kiss me."

Nick frowned. "I did want to kiss you, I wasn't the one who ran away when it was getting good."

"You really wanted it?"

"Yes, I'd fallen for you and your positivity, and your sense of humor, and I really wanted to taste you."

"Oh, I thought…" Cameron didn't finish. What was the point in rehashing the past when the present was offering a kiss.

"It was good you left, I think."

"Why?" Nick didn't run at that announcement, simply pressed his face against Cameron's hands and smiled.

"Because what I had was a stupid kid's crush, but this is different, and I can probably kiss a lot better now."

Nick smirked. "You had a lot of practice?"

"Enough so I don't suck." Cameron rubbed his thumb on Nick's cheekbone.

"I quite like sucking. But maybe you'd better show me how practice has helped. I mean, I remember the kiss—it was hot."

Cameron shook his head as Nick placed one hand on

the door and the other on Cameron's hip. "It was all tongue and flailing. I remember it well."

Cameron slid his hand down and around the back of Nick's neck, settling his fingers into the soft hair at the nape.

Nick stepped a little closer. "All I recall is that it was hot, and you were into me for some strange reason, and I was leaving the next day. It seemed like a good idea to get one first, final thing for me to take with me. Selfish, I know. Then I kissed you, and it was everything I'd thought it would be."

Nick pressed a soft kiss to Cameron's lips and pulled back, and there was that smile again, the one that lit up his normally serious dark eyes and made Cameron fall for him all over again. For a moment, they looked at each other.

"We're doing this," Nick said. But he needed to ask one more thing. "How drunk are you?"

"I'm not."

"Hmmm."

"I'm not. Fuck, Nick, I've lusted over you since I was thirteen, for God's sake. You're here, I'm here—"

Cameron didn't finish the sentence because the alcohol and the excitement were stealing all his rational thoughts away. And wait… had he just admitted he'd lusted after his best friend's older brother from the age of freaking thirteen?

*Fuck my life.*

Nick didn't seem bothered; he leaned in for another kiss, and this time he pushed for more. And Cameron was only too happy to go with the flow. The kiss was everything he remembered, the taste, the urgency, the way

Nick covered him and held him and made him feel protected and safe.

Then there was more: the new parts, the sex, the need, the scorching heat, and the way Nick didn't let up as they kissed. Cameron curled his other hand into Nick's hair and widened his stance a little so that Nick could slot between them. Nick shuffled even closer, his hands on Cameron's ass, holding him as close as possible.

Nick was hard against him, and with enough friction, Cameron could get off like this, standing against their room door and kissing until they came.

Seemed like Nick had other ideas, though. He stepped back, not breaking the kiss. They both shoved at jeans and shirts, and each time someone managed to remove something, they went back to the kiss. Finally naked, Nick tumbled them both onto the nearest bed, and then somehow they scooted up so that Cameron was lying half on Nick and half off. Nick shifted slightly, until the only comfortable position Cameron could find was with his leg draped across Nick's thigh. He could feel every inch of Nick.

"I don't know what to do next," he murmured, "It's like I have everything I want right here, and I don't know where to start." He smiled down at Nick, embarrassed and oddly emboldened at the same time.

The new position put him firmly in control of whatever the hell he wanted to do next, and Cameron knew what that was: skin on skin, and laughter, and more kisses, and he wanted this to be more than one night. He pulled back from the kisses a little. "What about tomorrow?"

Nick looked puzzled. "Tomorrow?"

"Is this just tonight? Because if it's just tonight then I

want to do everything, but if you can give me another night, I can spend my time kissing you everywhere because I know I'll get another chance at the rest."

An unidentifiable expression passed over Nick's face. Cameron tensed.

"Actually," Nick began softly, "I was hoping for more than just a couple of nights."

Cameron's heart lifted. "Really?"

"Maybe until we get to the wedding. I don't know. We might be awful together in bed." Nick must have seen Cameron's expression tighten a little because he quickly added, "But it's been perfect so far."

Cameron rested his gaze on Nick's stubble-rough skin and the pulse in his throat.

"Cameron?" Nick prompted. "Is that okay?"

Cameron groaned and dropped his head into the hollow of Nick's neck. "God, yes. I want to…." He'd talk Nick around when they reached the wedding. There was no need for endings.

"Yeah," Nick murmured.

Somehow that was the entire conversation. Cameron whimpered into Nick's skin.

"It's good. We can have fun," Nick said.

Cameron pressed a kiss to Nick's pulse, then back to his lips, and they kissed deeply. The kissing soon became more: explosive, clashing, needy, hard. Cameron laced his fingers with Nick's and unconsciously tightened his grip, pressing down harder, and Nick groaned.

Nick unlaced their fingers and instead placed his hands firmly on Cameron's ass, shifting him slightly, rolling them together, setting a rhythm.

Cameron was so close, and in a desperate move, he

ripped himself out of Nick's hold and sat up on his knees, closing his hand around his cock. He closed his eyes.

"Cam?"

"Just give me a minute." Cameron leaned over for more kissing, pressing a hand to his cock, wanting to stop the inevitability of the orgasm that had him wanting to come like the teenager he'd been at that party. He moved again, straddling Nick and kissing down his chest to his hipbones, biting the skin stretched there, then kissing across to Nick's cock. He didn't hesitate there; Cameron wanted a taste of something he'd only imagined.

He wasn't disappointed. Particularly when Nick's hands twisted in his hair and held him still.

"Fuck, Cameron," Nick groaned.

Cameron didn't stop, lowering his mouth on Nick's length, setting a rhythm and copying the movement with his hand on his own cock. Nick's hands tightened in his hair, not pushing, but the prickle of pain was enough to sweep Cameron's orgasm over him. His release spattered on Nick's thigh.

"I'm coming."

Nick's voice broke, but Cameron didn't move, swallowing Nick's spend and then licking his way up Nick's body until he lay spread-eagled over his new lover.

"I've never—never felt—" Cameron stuttered and then said nothing else.

"Cameron? That was…." Nick sounded as out of it as Cameron was.

Cameron rolled off and padded to the bathroom, grabbing tissues and bringing them back into the room. He couldn't help grinning at Nick's loose spread of limbs in the bed. Nick looked at him with a soft smile.

He cleaned Nick up and didn't argue when Nick grabbed a hand and pulled him down next to him. Somehow they ended up under the covers. Nick turned with his back to Cameron, snuggling back as the little spoon.

Kissing, coming, and now spooning? *Perfect.*

## Chapter Ten

"So, are we going to talk about what happened last night or...?" Nick rested his head in his hand against the car door and side-eyed Cameron.

Cameron didn't say anything, focusing on the road ahead.

"Okay. Guess we're just going to ignore it."

"I don't know what to say." Cameron turned his head briefly. "Besides, I think I said way too much last night."

"It was kind of sweet." It hadn't done his ego any harm to hear how Cameron had viewed him growing up.

Cameron gave a heavy sigh. "It was embarrassing, that's what it was. That's why I don't drink much."

"Or don't drink around guys you've been crushing on since you were thirteen?"

There was a brief silence, but the moment lightened when Cameron smiled. "I'm never going to live that down, am I?"

Growing up, Nick had never viewed Cameron in the same way Cameron viewed him. Cameron was his kid sister's best friend. To even consider it back then would have been weird. But then there had been that kiss... their first kiss. Wet and awkward and secret. Or as secret as anything could be when Cameron's best friend was Kaitlin. Her less than subtle hints and how she kept dropping Cameron into conversation made it clear she knew.

For Nick it had been a half-drunken kiss with a cute guy, and what had it mattered? After all, Cameron had soon put a stop to it. And Nick had been about to sign up and be shipped out to who-knew-where. "I might find a way to drop it into conversation now and again," he teased.

"Thanks." Cameron still looked a little embarrassed but snorted a laugh as he straightened in his seat.

"You okay?"

"Just a little stiff, my muscles ache." He looked out the front of the car. "C'mon Mount Rushmore, you're a freaking mountain, surely we're supposed to be able to see it from the road?"

They passed a line of trees. Nick leaned his head and watched scenery as they drove by. "I have no idea."

He had decided to stick to the original plan for the day, the one Kaitlin and Cameron had made between them. He'd never been to Mount Rushmore and didn't think he would ever make the journey himself. Not anytime soon, anyway.

"Okay." Cameron seemed to be talking to himself as he guided the vehicle into the marked lane. He followed the road around the corner and slowed when he spotted the booths and barriers. "You got any change?"

Nick glanced at the parking prices. "Sure." He lifted his hip and pulled out his wallet.

Once through the barrier, Cameron followed the road. "Okay, guess we can go now."

"What?" Nick looked out the window, spotting the sculpted mountain in the distance.

"Well, we've seen it now, right?" Cameron laughed. His turn to tease.

*Nice try, Cam.* "I don't think so. I've just paid for parking, so we're going to park." Nick stared at Cameron until he glanced briefly in his direction. Nick grinned and folded his arms, sinking a little in his seat in faux protest.

"I guess it'd be nice to stretch my legs, get some air."

"Yeah, and spend time with your crush." There was still plenty of mileage and fun to be had with Cameron's admission.

Cameron opened his mouth, letting out a breathy sound, then shook his head. "I hate you."

Nick tilted back his head. "Nah, you love me."

Cameron snorted a laugh, then pressed his lips into a thoughtful pout, focusing on the directions to the parking area.

With a smile, Nick stared out the window, examining the trees and the intermittent appearance of Mount Rushmore from between breaks in the stretch of forest. He sat up, suddenly thinking the carved faces had their eyes on him, as though they were judging him in some way for not getting his life together.

*What is wrong with you?*

It wasn't as though anyone expected him to carve a sixty-foot-tall head into a cliff face. He should be able to get his shit together; he just needed to figure out what was stopping him.

"Right." Cameron parked. "Ready for our next

adventure?" He reached between the seats and grabbed his camera from the space behind Nick's seat. "Thought we could walk to the monument, then maybe check out the café and gift shop."

"So, what movie has this place featured in?" Nick nodded toward Cameron's camera.

"Seriously?"

Nick shrugged. "You may have noticed I'm not the best with movie trivia."

"*North by Northwest*."

"Never heard of it."

Cameron looked a mix of amused and appalled. "The Hitchcock movie. Cary Grant."

"Yeah, not really helping. *Psycho* is probably the only Hitchcock film I know, and even then I've only seen the remake."

With a hand clutched to his chest, Cameron exited the car. "Wow."

Pushing open the passenger door, Nick joined Cameron outside.

"You must know other Hitchcock films. How about *The Birds*?"

Nick nodded. "Yeah, I think I've heard of it."

"*Vertigo*?"

"Is that the one with the guy who's laid up and spies on his neighbors? Because I have actually seen that one."

"No, that's *Rear Window*." Cameron chuckled. "You're terrible at this."

"I know, I know." He waved a hand, dismissing Cameron's observation. "Sitting around watching movies and TV has never been my thing. Not now or growing up. I mean, kids should be outdoors, right?"

A visible tension washed over Cameron as he averted his eyes. "Yeah, playing sports and building forts." He seemed to force a smile. "We should probably…." He waved a hand toward the trail.

"Yeah. Yeah, of course. Lead the way." Guilt ached in Nick's stomach as he thought back to his childhood, to Cameron's. It felt like a lifetime ago when he was hugging his twelve-year-old sister close, telling her that her best friend was going to be fine, that Cameron would beat the cancer. She would leave the house, a bundle of DVDs in her arms because that was all Cameron could muster the energy to do. No outdoors, no soccer at the park.

*Idiot.*

He didn't follow Cameron straightaway, allowing the space between them to grow. Things had already felt strained since last night and the discussion over Cameron's hair. Another comment about the cancer and Cameron would regret the two of them hooking up.

"Nicky, you coming?"

Nick blinked, refocusing. Cameron was looking at him with a curious but amused expression. Suddenly things felt easier, lighter again.

"It's just Nick," he said, smiling when Cameron did. He jogged the short distance to be at Cameron's side. Glancing at him, he got a sense of why Cameron seemed to go from one adventure to another. Zip wires, horse riding, all the places he'd been with Kaitlin… maybe Cameron was making up for those lost teen years.

"So, not Nicholas?" Cameron asked.

With a laugh, Nick shook his head. "Only my dad calls me that, and when he does it usually means I'm in trouble or he needs a favor." He crammed his hands in his jacket pockets and looked up at the clear blue sky. "Do you think it will snow tonight?"

The weather forecasts had promised snow the next couple of days. Though Christmas and its commercialism wasn't Nick's thing, he did love snow. He imagined a blanket of white and the feeling of innocence and fresh starts it conveyed as it covered the ground.

"If it does, I hope it's light. I could do without being snowed in the hotel with you."

"What's wrong with me?"

Cameron shook his head. "I didn't mean *you*, you. I just meant the room." He shrugged. "I'd go crazy stuck inside, and you definitely wouldn't want to see that."

"I don't know. It might be fun."

Cameron chuckled. "Oh yeah, quite the experience." He stopped as they reached the start of the trail to the monument and turned to Nick. "We're okay, aren't we?"

Nick wasn't sure what Cameron was getting at. "What do you mean?"

"You know, about last night and… us. I know I said some stuff and we…. But I get that it was maybe a one-time thing." His gaze lingered on Nick's. When Nick didn't say anything, Cameron started to walk away. "Or not. Hell… whatever."

"Wait, Cam." Nick caught Cameron by the wrist. "Last night was weird." A look of disappointment passed over Cameron's face. "Weird in a good way."

"Okay."

Nick released him. "You spent so much time at our house with Kaitlin when you were a kid, it was like I had a little brother."

Cameron quirked an eyebrow. "Okay, now you're definitely making it weird."

"No, I mean I just never thought about you *that* way." He shrugged. "Look, I'm not good at this kind of stuff. Words, I mean."

Lowering his gaze, Cameron insisted, "It's fine. Let's chalk it up to alcohol."

"A one-time thing? What about what we said, about…?"

Cameron tilted his head and nodded. "Yeah. A one-off or something."

But the tone of Cameron's voice was telling.

"What if it didn't have to be?"

It had been five months since Nick had split from Billy. In some ways he missed being wanted and having someone to share his life with. He met Cameron's eyes, holding his gaze. He had never really looked at Cameron before, not in the way he was now. The man was gorgeous, but it was more than that. Spending time with Cameron was easy, and though he might not say it out loud, Nick enjoyed his company and felt good around him, no matter what adventure they had lined up.

Nick chewed on his lip. "What if I didn't want it to be?"

Cameron curled his fingers against the material of his jacket. "I don't know." He seemed unsure; there was clearly something on his mind.

"Is it because of Kaitlin?"

"What? No."

*Maybe he's not over someone.* "Your ex?"

Cameron gave a humorless laugh. "God, no." He

shifted his weight to his other foot. "Travis was a huge mistake. Time I won't be getting back."

The comment was strange to Nick, intentionally laced with a bitter tone.

Cameron added, "I'm guessing Kaitlin didn't fill you in on what happened?"

Nick shook his head. "I know you split."

Cameron breathed in deeply as if bracing himself for a difficult conversation. His attention suddenly flicked to the side, where an elderly couple outfitted with walking boots and thermal jackets made their way toward them and the trail. Cameron nodded in greeting and stepped out of the way. "How about we talk about it later?"

"Whatever you want. But it's none of my business. You don't need to tell me anything."

"No. I'd like to explain." Cameron watched the couple. "Just not now."

With a nod, Nick accepted Cameron's need to move on from the subject of his ex. "How about we get ahead of those two? Wouldn't want them beating us to the best viewpoints."

Smiling, Cameron straightened the strap of his camera and untangled his jacket's twisted collar. "They did look like they meant business."

Nick looked down. He was dressed in sneakers and jeans. "How long is this trail again?"

"Only half a mile or so." Cameron grinned. "You can put your Marine stuff into action."

"Marine stuff."

"Your training." Cameron laughed and it lit his face. "Whatever. You coming?"

Nick lowered his gaze for fear he might lose himself in

Cameron's eyes. He didn't understand where the feelings had come from; maybe they'd always been there just off to the side and out of sight. He held out his arm. "Lead the way."

"HEY, YOU SEEN THIS?"

Nick placed the teddy bear back on the gift shop shelf and quickly checked out the rest of the store. Souvenirs weren't really his thing, but Cameron had convinced him to come in with the promise of treating him to a mug of hot chocolate from the café. Nick crossed the store to stand behind Cameron and peer over his shoulder.

On a large notice board was an array of flyers. The poster Cameron had taken an interest in was for another escape-room experience.

With a snort, Nick said, "I don't think so. One escape is plenty."

"But it's a Western saloon!" Cameron cast Nick a sideways look. "Okay, maybe not." He checked around. "Think I'm going to see if there's something tacky to get your sister."

"Knock yourself out." Nick turned back to the board of pinned brochures and advertisements. Scanning them, his attention was drawn to the image of a hot-air balloon.

On the other side of the store, Cameron was picking up various items, turning them over in his hand, then replacing them, seemingly unsatisfied by their level of tackiness.

Nick smiled and picked up one of the leaflets for the hot-air balloon experience from the shelf beneath the board. Skimming the text, he eyed the digits on the back of the flyer. The flyer advised bookings be made well in advance as slots filled up quickly.

"What are the chances?" He looked back at Cameron. They'd made a deal to do what Nick wanted, and he couldn't shake the idea. Pulling out his cell phone, he headed for the door. "I just need to make a call."

He didn't hear Cameron's reply properly because the exit door creaked when he opened it and again when he let it swing shut after him. He tapped digits into the phone and waited.

A woman answered. "Hello, this is Full of Hot Air Rides. May I help you?"

"Hi," he said. "I know this is a long shot, but I'm only in town for the night. Do you have a slot available to fly tomorrow morning?" Mentally he crossed his fingers and waited.

"You're in luck. Our booking cancelled for tomorrow."

"Seriously?"

"The threat of snow dissuaded them from venturing this way. I have to warn you that depending on weather conditions, it may be us doing the cancelling this time." She already sounded apologetic. "I would suggest calling to check if things are going ahead. I'll give you the details of your pilot. You can contact him before heading out."

"No, that's great."

The woman rattled off details; what time sunrise was, when and where they would be picked up, what to wear, who their pilot would be, and how to make payment.

Nick repeated the information back to her. The creak of the gift shop door made him turn around. He raised a hand, indicating the call was almost over.

"Tomorrow about six. Thank you," he said and hung up.

Cameron stepped down off the wooden porch. "Kaitlin?"

"No. I was arranging something for tomorrow morning."

"What kind of something?"

Nick pursed his lips. "It's a surprise."

Cameron folded his arms. "I'm not sure I like the sound of that."

"Scared?"

"No. I just like to be prepared."

"In that case you might want an early night. We need to head out a little after five."

Curling his top lip, Cameron looked disgusted at the thought. "In the morning? As in a.m.?"

With a nod, Nick turned on his heel and headed in the direction of the café. "But first, you owe me a hot chocolate." He looked back over his shoulder when Cameron didn't follow straightaway.

"Five in the morning?" Cameron said again.

"It'll be worth it, I promise."

Cameron looked thoughtful. "You're really not going to tell me?"

Nick grinned. "Nope."

## Chapter Eleven

"THAT'S GREAT. THANK YOU. SEE YOU IN A LITTLE while."

When Nick ended his call, Cameron buried his head in his pillow. Sure, he'd had plenty of early starts working on movie sets, but he was supposed to be on *vacation*. Kind of. He didn't really see the book and photography so much as work but as a project, an indulgence.

"Hey. Time to get up."

"Leave me here." He'd heard Nick's alarm go off three, maybe four times after Nick had repeatedly hit the snooze button. "Save yourself."

Nick sighed loudly and pulled at the covers Cam had wrapped himself tightly in. "You made a deal, mister." He yanked harder. "We're doing this."

*Doing what, exactly?* Despite pressing him last night, Nick hadn't budged. Must have been more of that Marine training that meant he wouldn't crack under interrogation.

Cameron held on to the covers. "What time is it?" he grumbled.

"You've got fifteen minutes to get your ass up and dressed." Nick tugged again, managing to free the comforter from between Cameron's legs.

"What do I need?"

"Just you." Nick pulled a little more firmly.

The bedding slipped from Cameron's grip. "Dick." He rolled onto his back. Taking his pillow with him, he hugged it to his chest. "It's too cold." He squinted and turned his head. "And way too dark."

"Cameron."

"Nicholas." Cameron quirked an eyebrow in response to Nick's attempted stern expression. "*Fine*." He flung the pillow to one side and sat up. "Are you at least going to tell me where we're going?" He waited expectantly, but Nick didn't seem ready to share his plans for the morning just yet.

"I'm getting us coffee," Nick stated, and without another word, left the hotel room.

Cameron took a deep breath, then reached over to grab his cell. On auto-pilot he went straight to check his email. There was one new message from the junior assistant who had been shadowing him the last couple of months, copying him in on some paperwork for a site that required filing.

He glanced at the time on the email. Two a.m. "Seriously, Josh?" He shook his head and turned off the screen. Placing his phone on the nightstand, he glanced at the door. Nick coming back and finding him still sitting on the bed in his boxers would not go down too well.

"Okay." In an attempt to feel more awake, he gently slapped his cheeks. "Clothes."

By the time Nick had returned with two black coffees,

Cameron had dressed. He sat on the bed to pull on his boots, eyeing the dusting of white in Nick's hair and across his shoulders. "It's snowing?"

Nick put the coffees on the dresser and dragged his fingers through his hair. "No. But it must have overnight."

"Then what's with the…?" Cameron indicated the snow in Nick's hair. He tugged on his other boot and got to his feet, grabbing his warm coat off the bed.

A sheepish expression crept onto Nick's face. "Did I ever tell you I hate children?"

Cameron raised an eyebrow. "Erm, no."

Nick nodded, his expression implying he wasn't being serious. "Yep. But I want you to know he threw first."

"Threw what?" It was way too early for being cryptic.

The look Nick gave him was laden with *isn't it obvious?* He pushed back his damp bangs.

"Wait. You mean you got into a snowball fight? With a *child*?" Nick smirked. "Why? How, even? It's, like, five in the morning."

With a shrug, Nick picked up one of the coffees and took a sip. He licked his lips. "I think his parents had released him into the wild for a little while after a long drive. On a pit stop or something." He took a longer drink of his coffee and then picked up the other cup, offering it to Cameron. "Something to wake you up."

Cameron rubbed his jaw, accepting the coffee. "Thanks." He held the cardboard cup, smiling at the heat against his palms, then took a drink and eyed Nick over the top of the cup. Nick pulled on an oversized beanie hat, and Cameron couldn't help but grin. "So, are you going to tell me?"

Nick shrugged and pulled a pair of gloves out of his

coat pocket. "Wrap up. Oh, and bring your camera." He took the car keys from the dresser and opened the door to the room. "I'll see you outside in five," he said and left.

Releasing a breath, Cameron stared at the back of the door. The talk he'd promised Nick about the situation with Travis had never happened. Truth was he hadn't known what to say, how not to make himself sound like a naive idiot.

*Because that's what you were.*

Cameron shook his head to dismiss the thoughts. That was not the headspace he wanted to start the day off in. Whatever Nick had lined up, whether it was a good idea or a bad one, Cameron was going to be positive and make the most of their day together. He wasn't sure what he wanted from this thing with Nick. Was it just some road-trip fun? Could it be more? He hadn't seen Nick properly in years, but laying eyes on him again had sparked his crush from way back. Nick was as gorgeous as ever, with a killer smile Cameron wished he saw more often. There was an edge to Nick, some weight he'd carried around with him since his time away with the Marines. But beneath the tough exterior—and certainly he'd seen glimpses over the last week—the same old Nick was still in there. A bit frayed around the edges, maybe, but he was there. And that Nick made Cameron feel things he thought he might never experience again.

Travis had worn him down, and for a long time he'd thought it was himself who was the problem. He knew it wasn't true, or at least, according to his friends he was supposed to know. It had been hard walking away from something that at first had been so amazing and passionate. Cameron couldn't remember when their relationship and

Travis' feelings had taken such a massive U-turn, but he blamed himself, and in some way it had made him feel unlovable.

*Shit, Cam, stop it!*

His mind had drifted to a dark place. He was done with letting Travis make him feel bad.

*Get a grip.*

Cameron took a long drink of coffee and gathered his things. He eyed his phone, considering the missed calls and unanswered emails still on the device. Travis might have been out of his life, but the inescapable consequences were not.

*One day you'll have to pick those messages up. You can't ignore them forever.*

Grabbing his phone, Cameron slipped it in his coat pocket and headed for the door. What did another day matter? Another week, even? Did he want to know? Have to know? Damn, he wished he could shut off his brain sometimes.

He pulled the door shut behind him, secured it, then walked the long corridor to the exit.

Today was going to be a good day. He just needed to put the crap to the back of his mind for a little longer. *Easy, right?*

"YOU OKAY?" Nick cast Cameron a curious look.

"What? Oh yeah, I'm fine." Cameron looked up at the rainbow-colored balloon as it filled with air.

"Not scared, are ya?"

Cameron's shake of his head was a little too animated. "Of course not. I'm just watching what's going on."

"You are, aren't you?" Nick laughed. "But what about all those pictures of you and Kaitlin rappelling and hanging off bridges and who knows what else?"

"We had ropes, and it was all very secure. There were safety precautions." The balloon was nearly fully in the air, the basket held down with weights. Cameron had never been this close to a hot-air balloon and he was strangely overwhelmed.

Nick rested a hand on Cameron's shoulder. "You don't think Horace has safety precautions?" He nodded in the direction of their pilot.

"A basket attached to a balloon hundreds, maybe thousands of feet in the air?" Cameron mused.

Squeezing his shoulder, Nick assured him, "If you fall out, I'll toss you a lifebuoy."

Cameron laughed and hugged his arms to his chest. "Thanks. I feel a lot better." He fell silent and watched their pilot do whatever checks he was doing. "So you know, it's not that I'm scared. I'd just let my mind wander."

Lowering his hand, Nick asked, "Go anywhere nice?"

"I can't remember." He was glad when Nick seemed to accept his answer. "So, how long will we be in the air?" He glanced up at the sky; a crack of morning light yellowed the otherwise gray expanse above them.

"Horace said it depends on the weather and finding a good landing site. Usually around forty-five minutes, though."

Nick edged closer, and Cameron noted the feel of Nick's shoulder. He smiled, comforted by having Nick close. He had seriously done a head-fuck on himself back at the hotel and was grateful for the distraction Nick provided and for how Nick made him feel. Happiness. Relief. That maybe he wasn't alone in all this after all.

"Fellas, she's ready." Horace tucked his hands in his pockets and stood tall.

Nick gave a short nod to acknowledge him, then looked at Cameron and smiled. "Wanna give me a leg-up?

With a sigh, Cameron gave Nick an exasperated look.

Chuckling, Nick held out his arm. "After you."


THE VIEW from the air was nothing short of breathtaking. Cameron wrapped his hands over the edge of the basket and took a long look at the stretch of snow-dusted forest that ran beneath them and toward the horizon. He wiggled his nose. Admitting defeat, he pushed his sunglasses up with a finger. The morning sun cast a beautiful glow over the earth, breaking through the haze as it rose above the trees.

"So—" Nick rested his hand beside Cameron's. "—did I do good?" He slid it closer until their fingers touched.

Cameron lowered his head and remained silent for a moment. Lifting his head, he said, "Yeah. You did."

A bright smile spread across Nick's face. He rested his hand over Cameron's, angling his body as Cameron shifted closer. He met Cameron's eyes, which held something deep and intense as he looked at him.

As Nick began to lean forward, Cameron straightened and turned his head, looking behind them to where Horace stood. For a moment, Nick looked disappointed until he glanced back at Horace.

"Don't mind me, boys." Horace flashed them a toothy grin. "I've been a pilot for thirty years. Reckon I've seen it all." He sniffed against the cool air and returned his focus to the path they were taking.

Nick smirked and leaned closer, angling himself to obscure Horace's view regardless of his kind-of blessing. "I've got to say the view up here is pretty amazing."

A sideways glance made Cameron aware it was not the scenery that had its hold on Nick. He breathed in deeply, the romance of the moment getting the better of him as he looked into Nick's eyes. "It's okay, I guess," he teased.

Nick edged forward and Cameron focused on his breathing. He smiled when Nick's mouth met his before losing himself to a lengthy kiss. The kiss was tender and slow, and somehow so much more than anything that had happened between them the other night.

Closing his eyes, Cameron enjoyed the gentle moment and remembered that being with someone didn't have to be as hard as Travis had made it. He let himself go and lost himself in the kiss. He hadn't been looking for this, for lust and the possibility of love. The road trip had been about putting Travis and their doomed relationship behind him, to quite literally move to the other side of the country. It was also about doing something for himself, to work on his book, see places he might never have gotten around to seeing.

A flash from the past unsettled him and he swore he could taste the stench of disinfectant at the back of his throat. He pulled away, catching his breath, and met Nick's eyes, The man anchored him in the present. Hesitantly he reached out, cupping Nick's cheek for a moment before leaning forward and pressing a kiss to his lips.

"Thank you," Cameron said, then lowered his hand.

"For what?" Nick turned with him and they looked back across the landscape before them.

Everything Cameron was running from felt almost insignificant on top of the great expanse of nature before them. "For—"

*For the balloon ride, for you being you, for being here. For everything.* "Just… thank you."

Nick nudged his shoulder against Cameron's, then rested his hand over his. "You're welcome."

"THANKS FOR OFFERING TO DRIVE." Cameron rested his head in his hand and stared back at the hotel.

They had gotten back from the hot-air balloon ride an hour before it was time to check out of their room. After packing up the last of their things, they spent the last of their time lying together on one of the beds. It had been kind of nice to lie there, no words, just the warmth of Nick pressed against his back.

"No problem." Nick pulled on his belt. "Sioux Falls, right?"

Cameron keyed in the details on the GPS. "Yep." He sat back in his seat. Yawning, he checked his phone as he had earlier put it on silent. There was a missed call from the clinic, and immediately the happiness of the morning was ripped away from him, the memories already tarnished.

"You okay?"

Cameron nodded and slipped his phone back into his jacket pocket. "Just tired." He sank a little lower in his seat, getting comfortable.

"Get some rest. I'll wake you when I find us somewhere for lunch." Nick gave an encouraging smile.

Cameron wasn't sure he could sleep in the car, but a chance to close his eyes and shut the world out for a little while sounded appealing. "If you're sure."

"I'm sure."

As Nick started the car, Cameron turned to look out the window. The snow that had fallen overnight was all but gone now the sun had come out, nothing but dark, wet patches on the road and sidewalks. For a while he stared at the trees they passed as Nick started the long journey to Sioux Falls. Cameron was too aware of how quiet it was in the car. No music, no radio host filling the vehicle with chatter. He glanced back over his shoulder. Nick was focused on the road, and Cameron couldn't tell if he'd bought the excuse of being tired.

*It's not fair on Nick.*

Today had been a good day so far. It had also been Nick's day. He had booked the balloon ride. Cameron shouldn't let one missed call ruin it for them. Making a decision, he shifted in his seat so he was sitting upright and facing forward.

"You not sleeping?" Nick gave him a brief sideways look.

"And leave you unsupervised?" Cameron teased. "I'm not letting you decide where we eat lunch. That last diner you chose was terrible." He leaned his head back against the headrest of his seat. "It was like eating rubber." Nick laughed. "I'm pretty sure the sausages could have doubled as dog chew toys."

"Wow, bitchy." Nick nodded in amusement. "It wasn't

that bad." He glanced at Cameron, who raised an eyebrow in reply. "Okay, maybe it was that bad."

The rest of the journey was filled with talk and a light mood. They made a couple of short stops along the way for something to eat and to stretch their legs, and after the second stop, Cameron took over the driving.

By the time they reached the city and found the hotel, it was evening. They checked in and hung out in the room for a little while before heading out for dinner.

"Bathroom. Be right back." Nick rested his napkin on the table and walked to the back of the restaurant.

Cameron watched him for a moment, then turned his attention to his phone. He'd had a second missed call while on the road, and this time there was a voicemail. Reluctantly he hit the keys to listen to the message, then lifted his phone to his ear. The voice belonged to a woman, some admin in charge of chasing him, reminding him his test results were in and he should arrange to come in, or he could call back between certain times and speak to the doctor over the phone. When the message ended, he replayed it, listening to her voice, her tone, her inflections, anything that might be a clue to what he might face when he finally went back.

Nothing. Not that she'd probably even know what the results said; that wasn't her job. Cameron raised his eyes, spotting Nick on his way back, and slowly lowered his phone, turning it face-down on the table.

From the look on Nick's face, he had noticed; as he sat back down, his gaze fixed on Cameron's phone. "Everything okay?" he asked.

"Hmm. Yeah. Work stuff." Cameron knew the

unevenness of his words sounded like a lie, glad when Nick chose to accept the explanation.

After dinner they headed back to the hotel. In the elevator, Cameron instigated a kiss, hoping for a much-needed distraction, but he was sure Nick knew how forced it was. There was worry, a slight hurt in the way Nick looked at him, and Cameron couldn't handle it.

As soon as they got back to the room, he got into bed, rolling away to put his back to Nick. He wasn't sure what he wanted Nick to do. Part of him wanted Nick to crawl into bed and hold him close; the other part wanted to be alone. In the end, it was down to Nick to decide. Cameron closed his eyes as he listened, aware of Nick getting into the other bed. As Nick turned out the light, he opened his eyes.

"Night, Cam," Nick said.

Cameron curled his hand in his pillow. "Yeah. Night."

## Chapter Twelve

NICK DIDN'T KNOW WHAT HAD CHANGED. THE BALLOON trip had been fun and, dare he say it, romantic. Even the long drive to Sioux Falls after had been full of teasing and fun. And then, last night, something had happened between dinner and going back to the room. Or maybe *at* dinner, because after dessert, Cameron had grown very quiet.

He'd said he was tired, but there was something else. Nick wasn't the most perceptive of people, but even he could see the anxiety that edged Cameron's actions and words until he chose to sleep in the other bed and gave a terse goodnight.

Cameron didn't seem inspired to stay in Sioux Falls for more than the night, saying that even though South Dakota had films like *Dances with Wolves* and TV series such as *Gunsmoke*, the locations were up in the hills. Instead, he said it was a chilly day and they should get breakfast and then make their way on to Rochester.

Once in the car, they talked and listened to music. Nick

managed to steal a kiss at the back of a truck stop, and hell, Cameron even kissed back.

"Is everything okay?" Nick finally asked when they sat in the diner at the truck stop, getting something to eat. Because if Cameron was second-guessing this road-trip fuck thing, then Nick would stop. It would be hard, but he'd give Cameron the space and wouldn't push.

Cameron looked up from his huge lunch plate of chicken and fries. He hadn't been eating them, just pushing them around the plate—yet another indication something was wrong.

"Sorry?" he asked.

"Was it something I said? Or did?"

"When?" Cameron looked confused.

"Yesterday. You've been… distracted."

Cameron looked back down at his plate, prodding a piece of chicken from left to right and back again. "I had a couple of missed calls and an email."

Nick waited for more, an explanation of their content or a reason why they upset Cameron. Looked like nothing was going to be forthcoming, though, so Nick concentrated on his own chicken and bided his time. He didn't push or ask any more questions, or even talk for the longest time, and finally he was rewarded with a soft curse and Cameron pushing his plate to one side.

"From the hospital, okay," Cameron announced and lifted his Coke, making a show of drinking, and not once meeting Nick's eyes. Then he very carefully placed the can on the table and folded his hands in front of him. "I had an annual checkup after some tests." Finally, he looked up at Nick. "I missed it, and they're chasing me. And before you say it, I know I should be calling them, but apart from feeling tired, I don't feel ill, and talking to them just means that I could be ill again. I don't want that again, Nick, so please don't judge me for not calling them."

Fear and compassion twisted inside Nick as he listened to the words tumbling from Cameron's lips. "Is there something... are you...?" He couldn't even form the words, had thought that after everything Cameron had gone through as a kid, it was all done now.

"Yes, no. Shit, I don't know."

Nick pushed his own plate to one side and considered what to say. Then he realized they were sitting in the middle of other tables—truckers, travelers, so many people —and abruptly he stood, throwing money down to cover their food. "Let's get out of here."

Cameron didn't argue, and they made it back to the car without talking. Seemed that the car, their home away from home, was the appropriate place for Cameron to talk. Snow was falling steadily, too soft to settle on the wet roads; even so it gave the impression of privacy as soon as they were both inside the car. Nick wanted to shout at Cameron, drag him to the closest hospital, demand he get his results. But, instead he aimed for understanding and compassionate.

"Do you want to talk about it?" Nick asked softly.

"It's Travis. It all started with him."

*Wait? What does any of this have to do with his ex-boyfriend?* Nick had thought this was about Cameron and the hospital, not the ex he would never talk about. "What do you mean?"

Cameron winced and looked away, out the window at the whirling snow.

"He was an asshole," he began, then stopped.

Nick considered telling Cameron that Kaitlin had told him the ex was a bastard, but instead he waited again.

"He cheated on me. You probably know that from Kaitlin." Cameron looked at Nick, and Nick nodded; he wasn't going to play games and pretend he didn't know.

"She told me he was an asshole. I'm sorry."

"There were other things that she doesn't know. Or at least she didn't know until I called her a few weeks back. I couldn't talk, and she freaked out."

"What couldn't you talk about?"

Cameron turned away again, looking pensive, worrying at his lower lip with his teeth. All Nick wanted to do was reach out and touch him, as if that might make this easier. Somehow, he knew Cameron was dealing with a heavy weight; Nick wanted to help. Hell, he'd do anything to get a smile back on Cameron's face. Ever since the balloon trip, he'd felt like he was on a precipice, at the edge of something very special, maybe a relationship that would make the decisions about Nick's future easier.

Right then he didn't have anywhere he needed to be. What if loving Cameron meant that he could just be wherever Cameron was?

*Love?* Where had that come from? Lust, certainly, but love meant more than sex and proximity.

Cameron cleared his throat and Nick pulled himself out of his random, terrifying thoughts.

"Usual shit people don't talk about," Cameron said. "Things where you have to admit you were less of the person you wanted to be. Not quite as perceptive as you should have been, or not quite as strong. The kind of talking where you admit you're a failure."

"I doubt you could ever be that," Nick said, with fierce loyalty in his tone.

"Travis liked to get physical, but not in a good way." Cameron paused and gave a sad smile. "I didn't let it happen much, but once, just once, he pushed me into a wall and I fell awkwardly, and it hurt."

Nick tensed, his hands going into fists; the ex was abusive? "Cam?" he asked, because he didn't know how to word what he wanted to know. Like an address, maybe, so he could go over and pummel this Travis guy into the ground, show him what real pain was.

Familiar anxiety chased his temper and he felt sick, aggression lay buried deep inside him, and he couldn't let it out now, not in the real world.

Except... this was Cameron, who looked like his life was ending.

"I left him. There was no way I was letting that happen to me. But the damage was done and Travis had chipped away at me. You get that?"

Nick nodded that he understood, even if he didn't entirely get it. There had to be reasons why a man as strong as Cameron didn't see Travis for what he was. Maybe one day they would talk about that as well.

"The way I fell, it must have done damage somewhere because the pain wouldn't go. So, I went to the hospital, saw a doctor. Turned out I'd fractured my ulna. It needed setting, and you know what that's like. The doctor was worried about my bones after he took my history. Not that anything showed on X-rays." Cameron looked so earnest, trying to convince Nick that everything was okay. "I had red flags on my file, and so when I went back for checks on the healed ulna, they ran some extra tests because I was tired, and dizzy sometimes."

Silence. A horrible, aching, poignant silence.

"What did the tests show?" Nick prompted, fear coiling inside him.

Cameron bit his lip, held it between his teeth, and stared right back at Nick. "I don't know."

"What do you mean?"

"I haven't asked them or spoken to the doctor."

"When were these tests done, Cam?" Nick reached out and took his hand, lacing their fingers and holding tight.

"Mid November."

"And you've avoided knowing them since then? Why would you do that? How can you do that?"

"It's easy to avoid real life if you want to," he began, sadly. "I've been in the car with just email and phones. I can ignore those, and ordinary mail will be at home." He held up his other hand to stop Nick talking. "I know it's stupid, I get that. When we go to the wedding, after I see Kaitlin married, I'll call them. I just want one last thing for myself before I find out what's wrong."

"I wasn't going to say it was stupid," Nick reassured, even though his first thought had been that very thing.

Cameron snorted. "What would you call it, then?"

Nick frowned. This was a test of how tactful he could be, and he wasn't known for tact. Then he fell back on the counseling he'd been getting; the information that made sense to him, anyway. He recalled the part about compartmentalizing everything in order to deal with what had happened, and how that was actually the wrong thing to do in certain situations.

"Call it survival instinct," he said. "You just want

normal, and you'll do anything not to face something outside the box." He looked out at the snow, trying to recall something personal that would make sense to Cameron.

"Sometimes I would wake up in post, and I'd think that maybe that day was the one I wouldn't make it back home. There would be death hanging over the camp, a friend from another team, or a guy I'd only met in passing who talked football with me, or the medic who showed me pictures of her kids. Some of those went out on patrol and never came back. I learned that if I focused on the what-ifs, I could make the here and now dangerous for myself. I couldn't second-guess what I was doing. Survival is focusing on the things you can control. So yes, I get it."

"Cancer isn't like being a hero." Cameron's words dripped with self-derision, as if cancer wasn't his whole world at the moment.

"Cam—"

"I'm just being stupid not calling for the results, but it's the only way I can wrap my head around my life. What if I leave it too long and I lose the chance to fight whatever is in me. I wake up sometimes and I know I am so fucking stupid. Then I think, I don't want to go through it all again. I don't want to be ill and lose years to this, I'd rather not know."

"Jesus, Cameron."

"I'm on this journey, taking photos, making something I can leave behind. Proof I was here, you know, for Kaitlin, or for anyone else who wants it."

"Stop that," Nick demanded instantly. "Stop imagining the worst."

"I don't know how else to do it. I've been outrunning

cancer since I was ten, and I can do that, you know. I can be the guy who takes the risks and knows all the movie trivia. The one who wants to love you, and he's a safe guy who doesn't have cancer."

Nick's chest tightened at the *love* part of that statement but he didn't think Cameron had even realized what he'd said. He looked pale and shocky, and Nick was out of his element. If Cameron used that word, and the same word was in Nick's head, then what did it mean? All he wanted to do was reach for Cameron and hold him tight, tell him that everything would be okay—lie if he had to. Anything to wipe the grief from Cameron's hazel eyes.

"Call them," Nick said. All the other options in his brain about what to say only led to a scenario with Cameron not feeling any calmer.

"No," Cameron said, unyielding. "I'll do it when we're in Vermont."

"Why?"

"Because a few more days won't hurt, and I just want this normal. Okay?" he said stubbornly, trying to take his hand from Nick's grasp.

But Nick wouldn't let go. "Okay. Let's look at it this way. You want this normal, this last few days before you know what's going on, and I can see why. But the moment you start thinking about it seriously, you lose perspective and you crawl into yourself, and then you're not living in the normal because you're afraid. Right?"

Cameron's mouth fell open in an excellent impression of a goldfish. He looked startled as if it hadn't even occurred to him. Hadn't he seen that avoidance was only okay if you could handle not knowing?

"Shit," Cameron murmured. Then "Shit," he said again.

They sat in silence a little longer.

"What will you do?" Nick finally prompted.

Cameron looked tortured; he gripped Nick's hand tight. "Just a few more days," he said in a whisper.

"Cam—"

"Please, let's just get to Fargo."

For the longest time they looked at each other, and even though Nick wanted to argue, he didn't. He started the car and pulled out of the truck stop. Even though he wanted to say so much he didn't, simply concentrated on the driving, until he couldn't stand the silence.

"So, what's in Fargo?" he asked. "Skydiving? Cliff jumping? Snake handling?"

Cameron said nothing for a few moments, then huffed a laugh. "I need to check the itinerary. Films, of course, and I don't know what else." He fiddled with the radio, tuning it in to some local station playing classic rock, and the talking was evidently done, underscored by Cameron pulling up the hood on his jacket, curling against the window, and looking out to the right, away from Nick.

Nick still had reservations; he desperately wanted to be more proactive, maybe even rip Cameron's phone from him and call the doctor himself. Not that anyone would talk to him, but still... was he going to be able to stop thinking about it?

Right now, he would give Cameron some time to think.

## Chapter Thirteen

CAMERON STRETCHED HIS ARMS ABOVE HIS HEAD, ARCHING his back up off the bed as he tried to push the ache of tiredness from his body. He felt good, happy, for a millisecond, and then the weight of what he'd admitted to Nick, about the tests, and the delays, hit him like a sledgehammer. He went from grief, to feeling like an idiot, to being in love, and then back to grief all in the space of a few minutes.

"Morning," Nick said from the other bed. He was sitting cross-legged on top of the covers in a pair of loose sweats and a white tank top. He held his phone in his hand, scrolling through something on the screen.

"What time is it?" Cameron asked, glancing to the nightstand in search of his cell.

"Almost eleven."

"Eleven? Why didn't you wake me?" He pushed himself to sit up against the headboard.

Nick shrugged, his gaze fixed on his phone. "You looked like you needed it." He breathed in deeply.

"Anyway, seems it's only fair as it's someone's birthday." He turned his head and held up his phone.

"What?" Cameron narrowed his eyes, adjusting to the morning light as he made out his Facebook page.

Nick flicked his thumb, scrolling through a list of messages people had already posted to wish Cameron a happy birthday. "You kept that quiet."

"I'm surprised Kaitlin didn't tell you."

"Oh, she did. She texted me this morning." Nick rested his phone in his lap. "Do we have plans to celebrate today?"

With everything else going on, his birthday and making an effort to celebrate had gotten a little lost. Not that Cameron minded; birthdays were a reminder of the passage of time, a countdown to death one way or another.

*Wow, Cam. A little dark there.* He rubbed his forehead, firmly massaging his temples. "I don't remember. Kaitlin might have come up with a few ideas, but I'm happy to do whatever."

There was a brief moment of silence. Then Nick said, "This is probably a dumb question, but was the movie *Fargo* actually filmed here?"

"A movie you know? It must be my birthday," Cameron joked.

"I know it. Was pretty good. I saw they made a television series out of it, too. Might check it out one day." Nick got off the bed and grabbed the notebook and map from the top of his case. He dropped back down onto the bed and flicked through the pages of plans. "*Unglued*," he read. "A craft market. Oh, and we're booked into a workshop at some coffee shop." He curled down his mouth. "Sounds like an easy day."

*Easy's good.*

Nick went on. "There's somewhere I want to go if we've time. Maybe this afternoon before the market. It's right around the corner from there."

"Sure. It's your trip too." Cameron smiled. "Would you tell me where we're going if I asked?"

Nick worried his lip. "Okay, this will sound strange, but it's a chapel."

"A chapel? Okay, but why would that be strange?"

"I don't know." Nick shrugged. "I guess I've never really talked to anyone about what I believe. Though I'm not sure I know what that is anymore, anyway."

Cameron cocked his head and let his gaze drift over Nick's face. He imagined that going to war could affect a man's beliefs and prayers. When he'd been ill, his grandmother always seemed to be praying for him, for their family. Sure, he had gotten better, but what about the children who hadn't, children who had been his friends? Why had the prayers for them gone unanswered?

"I don't think it matters what you believe in, so long as you believe in something. God, unicorns, coffee." Cameron grinned as Nick turned his head. "How about I let you treat me to a very late breakfast, and then we can go and find this chapel of yours."

"Deal."

They headed downtown, finding a small out-of–the-way café.

Nick held up his phone. "Is that really you? Look at those bangs."

Cameron took a mouthful of omelet and leaned forward. He chewed and swallowed, half coughing as he saw the photograph his mother had somehow managed to share to his profile. "Oh, my God. Whoever taught her how to use a computer needs shooting."

"How old are you there?"

The picture was an old school photo. "It's from fourth grade I think." He took Nick's phone from him. "Yeah. I think I was ten." He handed back the cell.

"You were adorable. I remember that."

Laughing, Cameron lowered his head and nudged a cube of fried potato around his plate. That picture brought back memories. It wasn't long after that photo when it became clear something wasn't right with him. He remembered always being tired, the headaches and vomiting, and the moment he looked in a mirror and realized he'd lost weight, how he could see his ribs beneath sunken skin—

"Wow."

Cameron raised his head, relieved to be pulled back into the present. "What?"

"Kaitlin's posted." Amusement danced over Nick's face.

There were so many embarrassing photographs of him that Kaitlin could share. "Dare I ask?"

Nick turned his phone around. "Is it wrong to say the seashells suit you?"

Cameron sighed as he laid eyes on the image of himself dressed as Ariel from *The Little Mermaid*. "I'll kill her." He shook his head. "It's from her twenty-first." He glanced at the picture again. The theme had been 'Disney characters', Kaitlin stood beside him, dressed in a lion outfit, her face painted in shades of yellow and brown. She posed beside him, roaring.

"It looks like you had fun."

Cameron nodded. "At least from what I remember. Never did find out where I lost those shells."

Nick turned off his phone and rested it on the table. "Wish I could have been there to legally buy her a beer or something."

"She's more of a cocktail kind of girl," Cameron said to comfort him.

Nick hadn't been in the position to just hop on an airplane for every family birthday and anniversary or for the holidays.

They fell into a thoughtful silence and finished their meals.

As agreed, from the café they made their way to the chapel Nick had mentioned. Standing on the street, Cameron eyed the simple building. It wasn't what he had expected. The chapel was painted off-white, and a wave-shaped stretch of windows in the pitched roof formed what Cameron assumed was a skylight to allow more natural light inside.

"If you don't want to come inside, I don't mind." Nick's breath misted in the cold air as he spoke.

"I'll come."

Nick smiled, briefly squeezing Cameron's hand before checking it was safe to cross the street.

Cameron followed, jogging to keep up.

In the chapel, the warmth was a welcome change from the wintry weather outside. They entered a large room and Cameron stopped. He glanced around the space. Three walls were covered in a series of canvas panels that together formed a large artwork. The piece was an abstract collage themed in red and orange.

"What is this?" Cameron stepped farther into the room and scanned the walls.

"I was reading about it online. A space to come and just be. Whether you want to pray, meditate, or think about life and your choices and stuff." Nick pulled down the zipper on his jacket and side-eyed Cameron.

"You mean about the hospital?"

Nick shook his head. "Not just that." He sighed. "I thought maybe... maybe I could find some answers for myself."

Pulling off his gloves, Cameron came to stand beside Nick and stared at the panel in the artwork directly in front of them. What was he supposed to see among the shapes and colors? "What's the question you need answers to?" he asked.

"More like questions, plural." Nick rubbed at his jaw. "Where's my life heading? What should I do? Where do I want to be?" He cocked his head as he observed the artwork. "Should I stay in Frosty Hollow?" He glanced at Cameron. "Or is there something worth going back to Seattle for?"

Cameron parted his lips, but he didn't know what to say. Nick's gaze was like a great weight on him. "Nick. I can't answer that for you."

"Sure, you can. I like you, more than like you, and I know you feel the same."

It didn't matter what Cameron felt for Nick. "And what if I do? I can't promise you us, or a future."

"Which is why you need to phone the hospital," Nick persisted. "Look at this place."

Cameron scanned the fifty-foot artwork. He focused on the curved wall, where numerous smaller canvases fitted together to follow the crests and troughs of the waves of wall. Whatever Nick saw in that place was more than Cameron maybe ever could.

Nick said quietly, "I'm not good with long speeches, but doesn't it make you think anything is possible?"

Cameron couldn't deny that the piece was impressive and must have taken someone a great deal of time, effort, and passion to complete it. "Maybe." He tensed when Nick came to stand in front of him.

Gently, Nick rubbed Cameron's arms, hooking his hands under his elbows. "Promise me you'll think about it? Please."

As uncomfortable as it was to admit, Cameron knew Nick was right. If he was ever going to move forward, he needed to find out what his future held. Good or bad, he'd deal with it as he had dealt with every high and low life had thrown at him so far.

"Okay," Cameron agreed, "I'll think about it." He looked beyond Nick, once more at the wall of art. "Promise."

Time seemed to pass quickly at the chapel, and it was late afternoon when they arrived at the next stop.

"Okay, the workshop starts in about fifteen minutes," Nick stated when they were inside. He glanced at a chalkboard behind the counter. "What's a Dala horse?"

Cameron read the board, which stated today's workshop was to carve a wooden Scandinavian Dala horse. "A breed of horse from Scandinavia?" he said with a shrug. "Sorry, I don't know." He smiled at the young woman standing behind the counter.

"Not a breed, no. It's one of these." The blonde barista placed a brightly painted wooden horse on the counter.

"It's an ornament, I guess you'd say. Paint it red and give it to your grandmother for Christmas. Or any family member," she quickly added.

"So, we're carving one of these?" Cameron picked up the horse and looked it over. "I don't see this going wrong at all." He placed it back on the counter. "Guess you know what you're getting for Christmas now, Nick."

"What? A three-legged wooden cow?" Nick beamed brightly, clearly finding himself funny.

"Would you like anything while you wait?" the barista asked. She seemed to be suppressing a smirk as she looked back and forth between them.

A warm drink was just what Cameron needed. "Sure. Two of your gingerbread lattes, please."

Carrying their drinks, they took a window seat, chatting idly for a few minutes as a handful of other people arrived for the workshop. Then the person leading the session came in, a middle-aged man called Bernie who sounded like he'd stepped straight out of the *Fargo* movie.

The workshop took place in a function room on the second floor, and Cameron turned out to be as terrible at woodcarving as he'd expected.

"At least it has four legs," Nick commented.

Cameron looked at the four legs, aware of how uneven they were. As he'd shaved length off one, it went from being the longest to the shortest, and then he had to cut more off the other three. He eventually reached a point where he had to call it quits with the legs, or the poor horse would have been left with four tiny stumps.

He eyed Nick's carving. Of course, Nick's was near perfect. "I hate you."

The workshop allowed up to three hours for people to

complete their carvings, with tips on how to decorate the horse at home.

"Happy birthday," Nick said as they left the coffee shop. He held out his finished horse.

"For me? You shouldn't have." Cameron took the carving. The figure was almost as good as the demo one Bernie had made. "Have you ever considered a career in horse carvings?" he teased.

With a laugh, Nick took back the horse and put it in his coat pocket. "I think I'll stick to cars and engines." He scuffed at the sidewalk, scraping away the light snowfall. Lights from shop windows and the occasional streetlight illuminated the otherwise dark street. It was after six, and the evening had crept in while they were inside the coffee shop.

Cameron asked, "Did you ask Jamie to see if his dad had anything?"

Kaitlin's soon-to-be father-in-law owned a cab company and had in-house mechanics.

"He offered, but he's fully staffed, so it would only be part-time. He said he'd pass my details on to some of his contacts. Not heard anything yet." They walked along the street.

"I wish I could help." Cameron pursed his lips. "Maybe I could."

Nick raised an eyebrow. "How?"

"I don't know anyone directly, but I could talk to my boss, and maybe he could see if anyone in the industry is looking for qualified mechanics."

"On movie sets?"

"Or TV. A lot of shows have cars on set. They must need people to look after them, keep them running."

Nick looked at Cameron curiously. "Is this you giving me a reason to come back with you after the wedding?"

Too quickly, Cameron shook his head. "No, I didn't mean…. I was trying to help." He scratched behind his ear, suddenly embarrassed.

"If you were being serious, then I'd be interested."

Cameron looked up and met his gaze. "I was. But I can't promise you there'll be any jobs."

"That's fine." Nick wrapped his hand around Cameron's wrist, guiding him toward the buildings. "I have something else for you too."

"It's not another wooden horse, is it?" Cameron looked into Nick's eyes. "Because I'm not sure I could contain my excitement."

In a single, smooth motion, Cameron found himself with his back to the building and Nick's mouth on his in a firm but tender kiss. He breathed in deeply as Nick pulled away. "Not a horse, then." He ran his tongue over his lower lip. "What now?"

"It's your birthday," Nick pointed out.

Cameron considered where they could go from there. There was a low ache in his chest, the desire to have Nick close.

*Maybe later.* The evening was still young and full of possibility. He pressed his hand to Nick's chest. "I think we should go to the market." He patted him on the shoulder. "Then to dinner, and then—" He arched his neck, planting a chaste kiss on Nick's cheek. "—maybe later we could do something definitely better than carve a wooden horse."

Nick smiled and took his hand, and they walked hand-in-hand the rest of the way to the market.

They stayed there for about an hour. For Christmas, the market was illuminated by candlelight, setting a romantic backdrop for shoppers. They heard carol singers around them as they walked between the various stalls. Nick insisted they weren't leaving until he'd bought Cameron something, so to appease him, Cameron selected a box of honey marshmallows.

The romance continued through the night, from the market to the restaurant and then back to the hotel.

"Happy birthday," Nick said as they reached the door to their room.

Cameron smiled, closing his eyes when Nick leaned in for a kiss. He curled his fingers through the bottom of Nick's hair and pulled him close. He pressed his body against Nick's, pressing him to the door. "Happy birthday to me."

## Chapter Fourteen

NICK SLID HIS HANDS UP AND UNDER CAMERON'S SHIRT, feeling the warmth of his skin. For a moment, he leaned against Cameron and settled his breathing.

"Are you okay?" Cameron asked, sounding concerned.

"Just need to slow this down, or I'll be coming before I get anywhere near you."

"You saying you can't get it up again?" Cameron teased.

Nick swallowed the accompanying laugh with a deep kiss. While they tasted each other, he slipped his hands higher and helped Cameron remove his shirt between kisses. Bare-chested Cameron was gorgeous, and Nick kissed every inch of skin he could find, even as he removed Cameron's clothes an item at a time. Half of the fun was unwrapping his own kind of present.

"Happy birthday," he whispered again and concentrated on playing with Cameron's nipple. Then he repeated the words as he did the same to the other. And all this time, Cameron writhed under his touch, holding on hard with his hands twisted in Nick's hair, and it felt way past awesome.

Nick pulled away a little and then tugged Cameron toward the first bed, stripping off the last of his clothes. Then he knelt on the bed and Cameron followed him.

"What do you want?" Nick asked. He needed to know what Cameron needed tonight.

"Anything." Cameron scooted closer to kiss Nick. His hard cock brushed Nick's and Nick inhaled sharply at the touch. How the hell was he going to hold himself back?

"It's your birthday," Nick began, but Cameron clearly didn't want to talk. He yanked at Nick and they fell in a graceless heap on the mattress, a tumble of arms and legs with Cameron on the bottom.

Nick straddled him, using his body to press him down, and he couldn't help the groan low in his throat at the proximity and the feel of Cameron under him.

Cameron smiled and arched up, then pulled him down so they could kiss.

Nick needed to pull back control if there was to be any chance of him not losing it in a few minutes, so he eased away a little and focused instead on giving Cameron the best birthday fuck ever. He kissed down Cameron's body, lingering on his nipples, hipbones, and navel, tracing the treasure trail of dark hair with his fingers and lips. At points, Cameron's hard cock bumped his chin and Nick deliberately rubbed up against the smooth, hard length of him, his stubble a soft abrasion there.

"Nick," Cameron whined. "Stop—"

Nick lifted up and away. "Stop what, Cameron? Licking you? Kissing you?"

"Suck me," Cameron pleaded.

"Jeez, Cameron, your voice," Nick murmured.

In slow, steady increments Nick eased closer to his target, nudging the tip with his nose and then closing his lips around there. He sucked and rolled his tongue over the head, and it seemed Cameron was lost for words because all he could do was mutter incoherently. He pushed his hips up, and Nick swallowed as much as he could, sucking down and using his hand to circle anything he couldn't get in his mouth.

"Your mouth—"

Cameron managed those two words and then went tense under Nick, using his heels on the mattress to push up.

Nick loved it, the power he had, the fact that Cameron was using his mouth, the way that he himself was so close to coming. Nick, swallowed more, tighter and harder, then released the suction, stopping to bite the soft skin of Cameron's inner thigh, sucking gently on his balls. Cameron cursed him and wriggled, but Nick pressed across his thighs, holding him still.

"Stop, please—" Cameron pleaded again.

This time Nick slowed everything down, reaching to the bedside table where he'd placed lube, kissing a pattern onto Cameron's skin as he rolled a condom onto himself, slicked his hand, and looked up at him, just to make sure this was what Cameron really wanted.

Cameron's expression was utterly focused, dark-eyed, and there was need written on his face. "Now, Nick," he said, less of a plea and more a demand.

Nick did as he was told, massaging, pressing fingers there, enough to slick everything he could. Then he paused. "How?"

Cameron lifted his knees, locking them with his hands. "Want to watch you," he said.

Nick nearly lost it again; the thought of pushing inside and fucking Cameron with force was front and center, but he wasn't that kind of lover. He wriggled up the bed a little, taking the weight of Cameron's legs on his thighs, and pressed forward as carefully as he could manage.

Cameron sighed and closed his eyes, gripping Nick's arms.

"Open your eyes, please," Nick begged.

Cameron opened them, looked right up at Nick, and smiled, a fond smile—and something inside Nick snapped. The careful control he had on the love he held inside began to loosen.

"Hold the headboard," Nick ordered. He loved that Cameron did as he was told, and the position extended the muscles in Cameron's torso. He was beautiful. Perfect.

Cameron groaned as Nick pushed inside him.

"You okay?" Nick asked as he moved.

Cameron nodded and didn't close his eyes; his mouth was slack with need as he pushed down against Nick until Nick was fully inside him.

"Fuck," Cameron moaned, "*Nick*."

"Are you okay?" Nick asked again. "Cam?"

Cameron moved one hand from the headboard down to his cock, circling it and gasping. "More."

Cameron was so hot and tight around Nick that he knew he wouldn't last long. He pushed Cameron's legs open wider and pressed even deeper, and all the time Cameron was talking, words of encouragement: *more, deeper, harder, fuck!*

Cameron settled into a rhythm, his hand still on his

cock, pushing down onto Nick as Nick pressed up; Cameron stared up at Nick and arched again.

"I need you to come...." Nick was so close, but he wanted Cameron to go first.

"Nick, fuck."

Then Cameron was coming, shouting his release, and shutting his eyes tight. That was all it took before Nick was coming too, losing himself in Cameron's heaving body.

"So good, so good...." Nick couldn't think of anything else to say. He wanted to say *I love you* but he wanted to say it with deliberation, not when they were high from orgasm. Instead he kissed Cameron deeply, and they laughed into the kiss.

"Fucking awesome," Cameron muttered.

Carefully pulling out as he softened, Nick then got up and headed for the bathroom. He cleaned them up before getting back into bed and manhandling Cameron under the covers. Then he kissed his way up Cameron's body to his lips, and for the longest time, they kissed. As each kiss became the next, Nick had to stop himself from telling Cameron how he really felt.

He wriggled to get comfortable, pulling Cameron to him and spooning him, holding him tight. He'd never felt anything like this.

*I love you, Cameron Bennett. Please be well.*

*Please don't leave me.*

Nick didn't say a single word of it, but he knew he was lost now. He was in love, and he wanted forever, and he'd been denying it far too long.

And if Cameron didn't feel the same way... then he'd learn to live with it.

. . .

THE JOURNEY from Fargo to Chicago was a relaxed trip, with a new peace between them. They took turns to drive and stopped a few times, mostly for snacks.

Their hotel was gorgeous, right near Lake Michigan, with views over the city. A good boutique hotel with old-fashioned ironwork everywhere and the biggest chandelier that Nick had ever seen hanging in the tall marble-floored atrium.

The bed was comfortable, and they didn't even bother talking about who got which bed, dumping their bags on one of them and falling onto each other in their haste to get to the making-love part of the evening.

They slept late on the eleventh, then ate breakfast in a small café close to the hotel, before doing the whole "tourist in a big city" thing. They decided the best way to see all of it was to take the open-top bus, so they wrapped up in so many layers that they looked like teddy bears. They sat in upper-level seats and watched as Chicago passed by. They alighted at the Bean, and Cameron took some artistic shots of their reflections in that and in the fountain.

They also stopped at Wrigley Field, home of the Chicago Cubs; the ballpark, according to Cameron, featured in so many films that he couldn't list them all. *The Blues Brothers*, which Nick loved, *Ferris Bueller's Day Off*, apparently a personal favorite of Cameron's, and a film that Nick hadn't seen called *A League of Their Own*.

"They won the World Series this year," Cameron said, looking up at the huge celebratory banners, but Nick could tell from his tone that he probably wasn't into baseball.

"Although how they can call it world series when it isn't the world competing?"

"More of a football fan myself," Nick admitted and then grinned. "Well. I follow the Seahawks, kind of. I'm as much of a fan as you can be when you only know half the team and have no idea who plays in which position."

"It's like we're kindred non-sports-watching spirits," Cameron said.

Nick couldn't argue with that.

On Nick's phone, they found a recommended restaurant for dinner because Kaitlin hadn't pre-booked. She'd made a note on the itinerary that today in Chicago was Photography Day.

Nick asked to see the details of the schedule. Cameron passed him a page from the notebook, and Nick borrowed a pen from the snooty-looking waiter after they'd ordered their food. He scribbled something on the paper and passed it back.

Cameron looked at it and snorted a laugh, clapping a hand over his mouth—but not before several diners had looked their way. He leaned in to Nick and said in a quiet whisper, "You booked us in for sex?"

Nick nodded, then frowned. He hadn't written the word *sex*, he'd written something very different, in his opinion.

"I didn't write that," he pointed out.

Cameron poked at the sheet. "Make love," he murmured.

Nick waited for Cameron's realization, but apparently none came because he looked at Nick blankly. In that moment, Nick knew that while he might be in love,

Cameron clearly wasn't. What they had done might have had the mechanics of sex, but to him there was love.

*We made love.*

Then Cameron winked. "Just teasing," he said, as if he'd been joking all along.

Nick smiled, but the smile didn't connect to any part of him inside. He felt a little lost, but thankfully had no time to think about it because the waiter came back with the check.

They paid and left, walking down East Walton Place to the hotel.

"I love this city," Cameron said, walking close to Nick, their arms bumping every so often. "Last time I was here, it was the middle of August and hotter than Hades, the hottest August day in years. And no wind. I was expecting wind."

The chill was definitely here now; snowflakes swirled around them, collecting to a thin layer on the pavement, mesmerizing in their gentle fall to the ground. Nick felt the need to say something poetic, to capture how he felt at that moment: the absolute certainty that he was in love and that they were together, and nothing could take that away from him.

"I want to come back one day," he murmured. *With you,* he added silently.

"A week isn't long enough here, let alone our few days now. I could set an entire photo book in Chicago."

"You should one day. I bet it would be popular."

"Hmmm," Cameron said.

That didn't sound like an enthusiastic yes. If anything, it sounded to Nick as though Cameron was imagining he would never get to come back to Chicago again.

He stopped suddenly. Cameron walked on until he realized Nick had stopped. Cameron was in the dark shadows between one street lamp and another, but Nick could still see the confusion on Cameron's expression.

"Are you okay?" Cameron asked.

"No. Stop saying that."

"What? Asking if you're okay?"

"Stop acting like you could never come back to Chicago again. Like you're dying."

Cameron's lips thinned and his open expression shut down immediately. He wasn't talking, defending how he felt, or telling Nick he was fine; he actually turned to keep walking, and Nick hurried to catch up with him.

"Don't walk away," he snapped, his temper just below the surface.

Cameron attempted to shrug him off, but Nick was stronger and way more determined.

"Let me go," Cameron said evenly.

"No. You don't get to walk away from me. Not after everything we've been through."

"Let. Me. Go."

"I can't—" Nick's voice broke; he couldn't hold this all inside anymore. "I love you, Cameron, and I won't let you give up like this, or hide, or stop fighting."

There, he'd said it. He dropped his grip from Cameron's arm, and that was it. Either Cameron would walk off, or he would stay and make things right.

"What?" Cameron sounded incredulous.

"I love you."

"You can't love me."

"I can."

"Nick—"

"Don't tell me how I can or can't feel." Irritation mixed into the passion of the moment, and he was losing control of this because Cameron was forcing him into a corner. So, he deliberately settled his breathing and waited for Cameron to say something else. Nick would not rise to this; he'd said his piece. Now he needed Cameron to let him know how he felt.

Cameron had said he wanted to be the man who could love Nick—had just thrown it into the conversation two days ago—but he didn't seem to remember that.

*Should I remind him what he blurted out?*

"Nicky," Cameron finally said, "really?" He sounded so confused, as if it hadn't occurred to him that someone could love him, or that maybe he could *let* someone love him.

Cameron stepped closer, cradling Nick's face. A group of people walked around them giving a couple of catcalls, a whistle. Nothing awful.

They were in the middle of the sidewalk with people there, witnessing Nick putting his heart on the line.

"I love you, Cameron. I have always carried you with me. When I was overseas, when I came back and saw your posts with Kaitlin on Facebook. I've wanted you all that time, and all that time I wanted to tell you, but only on this trip have I realized that I'm good enough, that I could be the one to make you happy. If you'll let me."

Cameron looked up at him, his tongue darting out to wet his lips, and then he pressed a cheek to Nick's left hand.

"We need to get those results," he said.

That wasn't exactly an "I love you," but it was a promise of sorts. Tonight, that was good enough for Nick.

When they got back to the hotel room, they made love with gentle tenderness and Nick told Cameron over and over that he loved him.

And it was beautiful.

## Chapter Fifteen

NICK BREATHED IN DEEPLY AND ROLLED OVER IN BED. HE felt nothing but mattress and opened his eyes. Lifting his head, he blinked as he searched the room. "Cameron?"

Alone.

Worry turned his stomach. Had he pushed Cameron too far? Maybe it had been too soon for dropping love on him. It wasn't as if Cameron had exactly said it back, after all.

*Crap.* He'd freaked him out.

The door to the room opened and relief hit Nick hard. *Cameron hadn't run.*

"That's great." Cameron said into his phone. He smiled as he caught Nick's gaze. "I'll get him to drop you an email. No, I appreciate it. Thank you." He lowered the phone.

"Everything okay?" Nick rolled onto his side and leaned his head in his hand, propping himself up.

"Yep." Cameron sat on the bed beside him. "So, that was Douglas James." He was looking at Nick as if the name was supposed to mean something to him. "I work for him," he clarified. "Anyway, I gave him a call."

"What about?"

Cameron raised an eyebrow. "You."

Waking up to find Cameron gone had unsettled Nick, and he was playing catchup. "Right. About a job?"

"Yes, a job. Now, like I said, I can't promise there will be anything, but Douglas is happy to pass on your details as I've vouched for your amazing work ethic and reliability."

Nick moved closer to Cameron, lifting himself higher. "Thank you." He smiled as Cameron leaned down and kissed him on the cheek. "You didn't have to do that."

"I told you I'd help if I could."

Nick rested his head against Cameron's shoulder and took a deep breath. He needed to ask. "Is that the only call you've made this morning?"

"Nicky…." Cameron looked down at him. "I'll do it, just—"

"After coffee?" Nick moved his head against Cameron's arm as way of comfort for both of them.

Cameron reached up and gently ran his fingers through Nick's hair. "I was thinking more once we get to Cleveland." He pressed a kiss to Nick's forehead. "Not an excuse. Just, it's a long drive, and if—"

"You'll be fine," Nick interrupted. He couldn't allow himself to think of any other result.

Cameron pulled away and sat up straight. He took Nick's hand in his and looked into his eyes, his gaze intense yet reassuring. "*If* something's wrong, I'd prefer not to have a five-hour drive ahead of me." He smiled. "That okay?"

*Cleveland is the next stop…* "Of course. Whatever you need."

Cameron planted a kiss on the back of Nick's hand. "Actually, I think I already have everything I need."

After coffee and pastries they hit the road.

NICK RESTED his arm on the side of the car. "Hard to believe it's been twelve days."

*Time flies when you're having fun.* Hard to believe he was, but true. He had enjoyed himself these last two weeks, more than he'd expected.

Cameron didn't say anything; he simply smiled, keeping his focus on the road.

Nick smiled. "You do this kind of thing a lot, don't you?"

With a brief glance, Cameron shifted in his seat. "What kind of thing?"

"Have adventures."

Laughing, Cameron said, "I like being outdoors."

"Hanging off rock faces and whizzing down zip wires." Nick idly ran the back of his fingers over Cameron's jaw.

"Yeah." Cameron said as he rotated his shoulder then gripped the steering wheel tighter. "Maybe I'm making up for lost time."

Nick cleared his throat. "Sorry. I didn't mean to…."

"What?" Cameron shook his head. "It's the truth. As a kid, all I wanted to do was what other boys my age were doing. Even when I felt okay, my mom never wanted me to go out. Always scared I'd get sick, an infection. As if the cancer wasn't enough."

"I'm sorry." Guilt caused an ache in Nick's gut.

"You really need to stop saying that." There was a light tone to Cameron's voice. "I realized a long time ago that nothing was going to change what happened."

Nick breathed deeply, resisting the urge to apologize once more.

"When I beat cancer, all I wanted to do was move past it, but I could see it in my mom's eyes and on the face of every adult who knew me. Sympathy and sometimes even fear."

"Must have been hard." Nick was lucky; illness had never affected anyone in his family.

"It was this black cloud hanging over me for a long time. But then I moved out, went to college, and it was me starting over. New friends, new job."

Nick snorted a laugh. "But you kept Kaitlin."

She and Cameron had been the closest of friends since they were small children.

Cameron nodded. "Because no matter what, the only thing I saw when I looked at her was my friend." He smiled. "Plus, she was the only idiot I could talk into doing some of that stuff with me."

Chuckling, Nick rested his head in his hand. He watched Cameron for a moment, tracing every line of his face with his gaze. Cameron looked well, healthy.

*He's going to be okay.*

Nick stared out the windshield, so many thoughts running through his head. Not only about his future, but Cameron's as well.

Cameron stated, "I really am going to make the call. I wasn't making excuses before."

"I didn't mean to imply you were."

"You need to know that this—*us*—does mean something to me."

The admission was comforting and Nick smiled.

"It's just…." Cameron's cheek twitched as he struggled to find the words he needed.

In the end, he didn't need to say them because Nick understood. The distance Cameron still held Nick at was more for Nick than himself.

Nick sat forward and rested his hand on Cameron's thigh. "It doesn't matter to me."

"If it's bad news…." Cameron shook his head. "I don't expect anything from you."

Gently, Nick squeezed his knee. "Maybe not, and you'll no doubt try and push me away, but I do love you. And I'm not going anywhere."

Cameron glanced over. He looked unsure for a moment until he caught Nick's gaze. Whatever he saw in Nick's eyes was apparently what he needed. "You wanna stop for something to eat soon?"

Nick leaned back in his seat. "Sure."

"TWO BEERS, PLEASE." Nick folded his arms and leaned forward, resting his arms on the bar. He tapped his foot on the footrest of his stool.

Cameron had made him leave him at the hotel, told him the call was something he needed to do alone.

Nick checked over his shoulder; he'd agreed to meet Cameron in this bar down the street from the hotel.

*Maybe I should have headed for church.* He wasn't sure of the last time he had prayed for anything.

The bartender returned and Nick paid for the drinks.

Nervously he picked at the label on his bottle. Every now and then, he looked at the door. He hated waiting.

Fifteen minutes later, the door swung open and Cameron entered. Nick examined each step, trying to read something from Cameron's body language.

"Hey," he greeted as Cameron slid onto the stool beside him. Nick waited for Cameron to settle before prompting him. "How'd it go?"

As Cameron swallowed, the bob of his Adam's apple made Nick nervous.

"Nick," Cameron began, his voice choked.

"Oh fuck. It will be okay. We'll do this together."

Cameron raised an eyebrow. "What? I didn't say anything yet. I'm fine. The tests showed there is no recurrence, just that I was anemic."

"Really?" Nick didn't mean to sound disbelieving, but Cameron sounded so *calm*.

"Yes, really." He tilted his head to one side.

Relief washed through Nick and he pulled him into a hug. "*Thank God.*"

Cameron pressed his hand to Nick's back and pushed his face into the crook of Nick's neck. "Thank you," he said.

"For what?" Nick asked as they separated. He slid a beer toward Cameron.

"For pointing out what an idiot I've been." Cameron picked up the beer. "I should have phoned them back straightaway."

"You didn't know what they were going to say." Cameron took a drink, then nursed the bottle between his hands. Nick thought Cameron should have been happier. "How do you feel?"

Frowning, Cameron shrugged. "I don't know. Kind of numb. I should feel—" He rubbed at his face. "What should I feel?"

Nick checked around the bar. Nobody was paying them any attention. He leaned a little closer. "You don't have to feel anything. Just know I'm really proud of you." Cameron gave a dismissive snort. "I mean it." He rested his hand over Cameron's for a brief moment. "Just agree." He grinned and leaned back. "We should celebrate. Some beers, a nice meal. My treat."

For a moment he wasn't sure Cameron would agree. "I'll let you talk about movies," he coaxed.

Laughing, Cameron nodded. "Okay."

THE EVENING PASSED in kind of a blur. They drank and ate, and Nick was true to his word and let Cameron share what he knew about movies shot in Cleveland. The only thing he really remembered from the movie conversation was that Severance Hall doubled for some foreign palace at the start of *Air Force One*. After that, beer had kicked in and his memory was a little hazy.

"Morning," Nick murmured into his pillow as Cameron rolled over beside him.

Cameron hugged Nick's waist, pressing himself firmly to his back. "Hey," he said in a dreamy voice. "What time is it?"

"Late," Nick managed. He'd fallen asleep again after turning off his alarm. He opened his eyes and stared at the light shining through the thin drapes. "I should probably shower."

"Mmm," Cameron managed and hugged tighter. "Probably."

"Or—" Nick wriggled until Cameron loosened his hold, and then he rolled over. "We could just stay here." He kissed him on the forehead.

With a smile, Cameron returned the kiss, pressing his lips to Nick's shoulder. "We could." He breathed in deeply, eyelids fluttering as he slowly opened his eyes.

Filled with a sense of peace, Nick ran his hand through Cameron's hair. He'd even dare to call the moment perfect. "I love you," he said.

Cameron leaned back so he could look into Nick's face. His eyes radiated the warmth of love. He carefully brushed back Nick's hair. "I love you too."

Cameron smiled brightly. When he said the words, it was like a weight lifted from Nick's heart.

The moment shifted to kissing, touching, and the gentle motion of their bodies as they pressed and pushed against each other. It didn't take long before Nick was coming. He kissed Cameron hard as he pushed himself into Cameron's hand with a low groan as he held him close and heat pulsed across his stomach.

"I love you," he said again and rolled Cameron onto his back. He kissed him, nipping his lower lip as he reached between them.

Cameron ran his fingers through Nick's hair, groaning softly as Nick stroked him to release. "*Nicky.*" His voice was throaty, rough. With a grunt, he twitched, spurting across Nick's hand.

Nick kissed him again before leaning back and meeting his gaze.

"What?" Cameron asked.

"Just looking."

Cameron laughed. "Okay."

"You're perfect."

Color flushed Cameron's cheeks and he shyly looked away.

Nick turned his face back and kissed him again, then gently rubbed his nose against Cameron's.

*As close to perfect as I ever imagined.*

## Chapter Sixteen

CAMERON GLANCED AT THE NEW EMAIL FROM THE CLINIC. Nick had taken some of their things out to the car. For the longest time he simply stared at the wall. He still couldn't quite believe he was okay. The team at the center hadn't been chasing him for a diagnosis of cancer.

Cancer wasn't even an option.

Which he would have known had he not put off the call for so long.

Cameron was missing something. He'd spent so long imagining the worst, that hearing he was actually anemic and didn't have cancer was something he couldn't begin to process. The anemia, they had said, accounted for his periods of exhaustion, the shakiness, and the aching muscles. They weren't worried it was indicative of any underlying condition; just announced it was likely a leftover from his childhood cancer. They had emailed him a care plan, a recommendation to keep in touch, and tagged on a Merry Christmas.

"It's not cancer," he said to the wall, as if he needed to remind himself.

The door opened and Nick walked in, a cautious expression on his face. "Are you okay?" he asked and then leaned back against the closed door. "Cameron? Talk to me."

"It's not cancer," he repeated to the wall, and then looked back up at Nick whose expression carried the joy that Cameron wanted desperately to feel.

Instead as he accepted Nick's reassuring hugs, Cameron's head was muddled and he shut down.

Bless him, Nick didn't say another word, didn't badger him out of his contemplative fugue state. In fact, Nick drove to their next destination, and Cameron spent a lot of the drive from Cleveland to Rochester, all four hours of it, silently contemplating worst-case scenarios.

Like the specialist calling back and saying it was all a huge mistake, and cancer was actually going to steal his life away again. Why wasn't his mindset changing; why was he expecting awful things to happen to him. He should be happy.

Hell. *More* than happy.

Surely getting good news was the best thing ever? He had Nick in the car, whistling along to a station playing only Christmas songs, and every so often Nick would look over and grin at him. Cameron always smiled back, but after a while, Nick's expressions became less certain. Cameron knew one thing with absolute certainty.

*I'm fucking this up big time.*

Nick asked him a full three times on the drive how he felt about the news, and Cameron had been honest: he didn't know how to feel. He needed someone to tell him how to feel.

They pulled into the Radisson hotel, in Rochester's central business district. The hotel was modern and clearly intended for businessmen, different from the ones they'd stayed in so far. Still, as Cameron recalled, it was right on the Genesee River and only thirteen minutes from the Strong National Museum of Play.

They booked into the room. Cameron excused himself for a shower, not even giving Nick the chance to say that he wanted to get in there as well. All Cameron wanted was the space to get his head out of his ass. For the longest time, he stood under the hot water, going over and over his thoughts and feelings, making no sense of any of it.

He was cancer-free, he loved Nick, they had a future together.

So why was he so overwhelmed? Why couldn't he get his head around it? And why the hell was he avoiding Nick?

He couldn't see himself in the mirror through the steam so didn't bother shaving, which was the only other thing that would explain him staying in the bathroom, so he made himself go back to the room. When he stepped out, with a towel around his waist, Nick was waiting for him, his expression serious, sitting on the bed. The position made Nick seem less intimidating, but even so, Cameron knew he wasn't going to get away with not talking.

"Spill," Nick said—or rather, he ordered in his sternest voice.

Cameron felt vulnerable standing there wrapped in nothing but a towel, water dripping from his wet hair. "Can we talk later?"

"No." Nick tossed him a small towel for his hair. "I don't know what happened in the car, but you went really quiet. So, if you're regretting us now you know you're okay, you need to let me know so I can put up a wall or two around my heart."

"I wouldn't do that."

"Seems like that is what's happening."

Nick sounded pissed. "Are you angry with me?" Cameron asked. "I don't want to make you angry, or to think I have any regrets."

"Then what's wrong?"

Cameron considered where to sit, because he really needed to sit down, and finally he decided he didn't want any distance between them. So, he sat next to Nick on the bed and bumped shoulders.

"I think I'm broken," he began with a huffed laugh. "I just found out I'm cancer-free and found the love of my life on a fantastic cross-country road trip of a lifetime. But all I feel today is like something heavy is sitting on my chest."

"Something like regret, then?" Nick asked, his tone careful. "About us?"

"No. God, no," Cameron said quickly. "Like it's all too good to be true and I'm waiting for the axe to fall."

Nick relaxed against him, then wrapped an arm around his back and pulled him closer. "I totally understand that feeling."

"You do?"

"We'll work through it together."

"I'm sorry." Cameron put as much feeling into those two words as he could.

"Want to do something to take your mind off things?"

Cameron pressed a hand to Nick's thigh. "I can get behind that."

Nick chuckled. "I thought we could go see the new superhero movie, get popcorn, and neck in the back row."

"Which superhero is it?"

"No idea, but there's always one out. You want to?"

Cameron rested his head on Nick's shoulder. Popcorn, a movie, time with Nick? "Perfect."

THE MOVIE WAS everything it had promised to be—action, larger-than life heroes, and laughter—and while they didn't get to neck because the only seats left were in the front row, they did eat their bodyweight in popcorn. At least it felt that way.

Back at the hotel, they fell asleep in each other's arms after some damn satisfying hot sweaty sex, and something lifted inside Cameron. *I need to learn to live in the moment.* He'd spent so long as a child wishing for the future that he'd forgotten about the here and now.

WHEN THEY WOKE in the morning, the sun was shining. Cameron turned in Nick's arms and cuddled in.

He could do this. He could be right here with Nick and enjoy every freaking minute of it.

Then it occurred to him. He wanted to tell Kaitlin. To explain how he and Nick had fallen in love. But he didn't want to do it over the phone; he really wanted to get to her place and show her how happy he was.

"I can't wait to get to Frosty Hollow," he murmured against Nick's warm skin.

"Me neither. I can't wait to tell Kaitlin her plan worked."

"What plan?"

"The one that she didn't share with either of us. The one where we drive across the country and fall in love."

"You really think she had a plan?"

"You really think she didn't?"

Nick rolled up and out of bed, and Cameron got a nice eyeful of his lover's awesome ass and broad back. As Nick padded into the bathroom, Cameron stretched under the weight of the covers, enjoyed the warmth, and sent up a quiet thank you for Nick's interfering sister.

"So, what's on the agenda for today?"

"National Museum of Play is just a short walk away, and a car-chase scene was filmed in Rochester for *The Amazing Spider-Man 2*, because the speed laws are less restrictive in upstate New York."

Nick chuckled and crawled up the bed, his breath minty fresh and his body damp from the shower. "I love it when you talk nerd," he said and trailed kisses over every bit of Cameron's skin not hidden under the covers. Then he peeled away the sheets and kissed the bits he revealed, until Cameron was writhing because Nick's mouth around his cock was the best thing ever.

Nick sprawled across him, sated—apparently he'd gotten off to the noises Cameron had made. Cameron held Nick close. "Think you need another shower," he said. "Want to share and conserve water?"

*Yup. Best. Morning. Ever.*

. . .

AS THEY WALKED around the museum, Cameron discovered so much about Nick. Hand in hand they talked about toys from their childhood. Unsurprisingly, Nick was all about G.I. Joe, while Cameron was more of a board games freak, not to mention his affection for Dungeons and Dragons.

They ate in the small café, sharing memories of childhood. Slowly the resentment that Cameron still felt about losing so much of his teen years began to filter out with the weight of extra memories. Like the Monopoly tournaments that he and Kaitlin had spent hours on, and the games Nick joined in, which were complete disasters because he bought everything without any regard for strategy.

"You remember that time Kaitlin sold you Pennsylvania Railroad for all your money."

"Stations are important," Nick defended.

"Thousands, Nicky. She bankrupted you in one go."

"Want to know a secret?" Nick leaned in and whispered, "I used to love getting you all riled up. You took it all so seriously, and you were so cute, all angry because I wasn't taking it seriously."

Cameron huffed. "You were teasing the sick kid?"

Nick sobered and hugged him, right in the middle of the Fisher-Price display. "I never saw you as sick. Just as Cameron, my sister's friend who got tired a lot and took Monopoly really seriously."

Someone tutted next to them and murmured something under their breath that sounded suspiciously like "a place and a time."

Cameron tugged away, planning to give the owner of that voice a filthy look, then saw she was a teacher with a class of tiny kids. Yeah, she didn't necessarily have an issue with them being two men, but perhaps only with coming across the PDA in a toy museum.

"Ma'am," he said in apology.

She inclined her head in answer and then smiled softly.

Cameron dragged Nick out of there and into the cold Rochester winter, but they were bundled up against the weather. They found the area where the car chase had been filmed; Cameron took some photos, and then they headed back to the hotel to pick up their stored bags.

By unspoken agreement they decided to skip sightseeing in their next stop, Albany. Instead they spent the evening holed up in the room with pizza and beer, looking at Cameron's photos so far.

Nick pressed the mouse to take him to the next photo. "You're very good." They'd already made it to Mount Rushmore, but hundreds more waited. Cameron worried Nick would be bored, but he'd made all the right noises, and of course it helped that they were curled up together in bed.

"Thank you."

Nick paused at the next photo, a close-up of him with the monument blurred in the background. "I noticed there are a lot of me," he teased.

Cameron felt suddenly shy. Yes, there were a lot of Nick, but at first Cameron hadn't realized what he was doing. It was only after the day at Mount Rushmore that he'd noticed how sexy Nick was in photos. He was the perfect model, all stubble and strong jaw, with those intriguing dark eyes and that look of confidence and restrained danger. He didn't say any of that, though. "I couldn't help it if you kept getting in the way."

Nick huffed and pointed at the photo. "Me. I'm in focus."

Cameron indicated the trash can in the corner of the photo, one that he would obviously crop out. "I was trying to take a photo of that can," he said. "It's a very nice receptacle for trash. Like I said, you just got in the way."

Nick scrolled to the next photo, him again. "And this one?"

"The sky. I like taking photos of the sky."

This went on, and they'd made it to Fargo when Nick finally closed the laptop and very carefully slid it under the bed. In a sudden move, he had Cameron pinned to the bed. Hands, chest, thighs, every part of Nick had Cameron trapped under him. He grabbed Cameron's hands and held them in one of his own, pinned on the pillow above.

"I'm charging you for every photo you have of me."

"I have a lot."

"Then it will be expensive."

"And what will each one cost?"

"A kiss for full-body shots, a handjob or blowjob for close-ups."

Cameron moved a little, hard cock sliding just right against Nick's, and Nick bucked up. "I'll make sure to count the photos."

They kissed, and Cameron felt cared for, and needed, and hell, wanted. Clinging to Nick, he lost himself in the sensations of making love to the man who'd accompanied him on this journey.

Cuddling, they talked about everything and nothing.

"What are we doing on our next stop?" Nick asked.

"I just really want to get to Vermont," Cameron said hesitantly. *Do I sound ungrateful saying that?*

"Actually, me too," Nick admitted.

So, that decision was made. They did, however, do a drive around Albany, locating the Route 787 spaghetti junction that had been used in *Salt*, the movie with Angelina Jolie. Cameron wouldn't bother with photos of roads. Lots of them all snarled up in loops. One day he'd hire a plane or a helicopter and do aerial shots, but today he would have gotten nothing more useful than pictures of concrete. So instead he took photos of Nick driving.

On the morning of the sixteenth, they left Albany and headed for their final four hours of driving.

To Vermont.

And, more importantly, to the small riverside town of Frosty Hollow.

## Chapter Seventeen

"KAY, YOU'RE SQUASHING ME," CAMERON MUMBLED INTO the crook of Kaitlin's neck as she held onto him. He closed his eyes and breathed in the sweet scent of her perfume. He smiled, recognizing it as the most recent birthday gift he had bought for her.

"We weren't expecting you for another couple of days." Kaitlin kissed him on the cheek.

Cameron pointed his thumb in the direction of the door. "I can go if you want."

Kaitlin rubbed his shoulders. "Don't you dare! I need you to save me from a prison sentence."

"Things going smoothly, then?" He chuckled.

"Mom's… being Mom." She shrugged. "But now you're here to keep me sane, and Nick's here to distract Mom."

Cameron cleared his throat as she mentioned Nick, and from the smirk that spread across her face, she'd noticed.

"How was your trip? Anything interesting happen?"

"Subtle, Kay."

"So, you and Nick are… what? Boyfriends?" She grinned and sat on the end of her bed.

When they had arrived at the Sheridan home, Nick had gone with his parents to get settled, leaving Cameron to catch up with Kaitlin. Cameron might have let his gaze linger a little too long as Nick had walked away.

"No. Maybe. I think so." Cameron sat beside her and blew out a breath. "We wanted to tell you together. Tell you your dastardly plan had worked out."

"You've had the hots for my brother since I remember. You guys just needed a push in the right direction." She bumped her shoulder against his. "And that other thing?"

Cameron nodded. "It's all good."

"Yeah?"

"Yeah."

Kaitlin rested her hand over his. "So, what's next for you two?"

The question had him stumped. He had his job, his life back on the other side of the country, and Nick? Sure, Cameron had made some calls, but there was no guarantee. Would Nick come back with him on the chance of a job? Or was it time for him to come home to Frosty Hollow?

"It's okay to not know," Kaitlin said when Cameron didn't answer. "Who needs a plan anyway, right?"

"You. And you can't deny it. I've seen your hundred and one notebooks you've filled just for your wedding."

She huffed a breath. "Okay. Maybe I do, but doesn't mean you need to have one."

"I know." He had done plenty of things in his life without thinking all that hard about them. Some he regretted, but plenty had left him with good memories. "I guess it's something we need to talk about." Was that a conversation he was ready for? The whole *Nick* thing suddenly felt way too serious.

Kaitlin prodded him in the arm. "Forget about it. How long are you sticking around for? Are you staying after the wedding?"

"I *plan* to head back on the twenty-ninth. Haven't decided if I'm driving back yet or dropping off the car and getting a flight." He ran his hand over his jaw. He hadn't shaved today, keen to get on the road and back to Frosty Hollow.

"I've missed you." She hugged his arm.

"I've missed you too."


NICK LOOKED around his old bedroom. Gone was anything that had made the room his. He eyed the beige walls and frowned when his gaze settled on a piece of art hanging above the guest bed.

He ran the strap of his bag through his hands. It didn't feel like home anymore.

"Hey," Cameron said from behind him. "You've not unpacked yet?" He nodded toward Nick's case by the dresser.

"Mom dragged me via the kitchen. Apparently I look like I haven't been eating enough." He glanced down at his stomach and gently rubbed his hand over his T-shirt. The last couple of weeks, he'd certainly eaten plenty.

Cameron stepped into the room. "I just came to say goodbye."

"You're going?" They'd spent so much time in each other's company that Nick was kind of used to having Cameron around.

"My parents are expecting me." Cameron gazed around the room. "At least you have a bed. My room got turned into some arts-and-crafts room for my mom."

"But you have somewhere to stay?"

"Yeah, they've a pullout couch, so…." Cameron stepped closer. "I don't know if I'll see you before the wedding, but I wanted to say I had a great time." He looked sheepish, almost embarrassed.

"A great time," Nick repeated.

"Sorry. That sounds stupid."

Nick moved forward. "Well, I had a great time too." He stood in front of Cameron.

"We probably need to have a real talk about this, don't we? Like how this is going to work."

"I know." Nick pursed his lips. "We could meet up one night. Dinner and a long chat."

Cameron smiled. "Okay." He leaned forward, planting a kiss on Nick's mouth.

The kiss was tender, loving. "I love you," Nick said as Cameron leaned back.

"Good." Cameron ran his hands up and over Nick's chest and gently caressed Nick's shoulders before kissing him again. This time the kiss was longer, firmer.

Someone cleared their throat and Nick opened his eyes. He met Kaitlin's amused gaze as she leaned in the doorway.

Cameron looked over his shoulder. "Right. I should probably go, but we'll do dinner, yeah?"

"Definitely. I'll call you later."

Cameron headed for the door. Kaitlin touched his arm and grinned at him as he passed by her.

"Dinner?" she said as she entered the room.

Nick faced the bed, turning his attention to his bag. He pulled back the zipper. "Yeah. We were going to talk."

Talking. Not his favorite pastime.

"Sounds serious."

He let go of the bag. He knew she knew about him and Cameron, but walking in on the kiss had to have cemented it. "He told you."

"I twisted his arm." She dropped onto the bed and pulled up her left leg to rest her folded arms on. "I'm happy for you." She picked at the stitched pattern on the quilt.

Nick narrowed his eyes and observed his sister for a moment. "What?" Something was bothering her; he could see that.

"Nothing. Just wedding stuff."

"Worried I'll upstage you?"

Kaitlin's lips curled as she seemed to suppress a smirk. "No."

"Cold feet?"

"Definitely not." She raised her head and gave him a firm look.

"Mom?"

Kaitlin sighed. "Yeah. It's not terrible, but she's always poking her nose in, commenting on everything. I did try and point out this was my wedding, not hers."

Laughing, Nick squeezed her ankle. "She just wants everything perfect for her little girl."

Kaitlin smiled. "Dad does say I'm his princess." She pulled up her other leg and sat cross-legged on the bed. Her expression became serious. "It's not just that."

"Then what?"

"You. I'm worried about you."

Nick coughed. "Me? I'm fine."

"You're making out with my best friend. This is not usual Nick-behavior."

Nick was confused. "Wait. Wasn't this your plan? Me getting together with your best friend?"

"Totally." Kaitlin sounded a little too pleased with herself. "I just never actually thought it was going to happen, what with all the thinking and brooding you had going on." She tilted her head. "You look better than you sounded a few weeks ago."

"I feel better, and I know you want to hear it."

"What?" Kaitlin looked at him through wide, innocent eyes.

"You were right." He met her eyes. "About the trip and about taking some time."

Excitedly, she grabbed his hands. "I told you." She drew her lower lip between her teeth. "What are you going to do now?"

There was a lot to think about, and it wasn't just about him anymore. "After the wedding and Christmas, I'm going back to Seattle." Cameron was going back home, so it made sense that if this thing between them were to stand any chance, he needed to return as well.

Or was that his heart overruling his brain? Was he okay being away from Mom, Dad, and Kaitlin? Why was he abruptly so sure that returning to Seattle was the next step he needed to take?

"You sure?" Kaitlin looked at him, putting a voice to his fears.

"I think I am."

*Way to sound unconvinced.*

"You think?"

"No, I'm sure. I don't know what will happen about a job, but if this trip's shown me anything, then it's that anything is possible."

If nothing came of Cameron's contacts, then there were more options open to him than just mechanic jobs. He just had to have the confidence to put himself out there and stop hiding from his problems. And maybe work on the relationship with Cameron; seize the day, be happy, or something like that.

Kaitlin leaned forward and knelt. She wrapped her arms around him and hugged him tightly. "I'm so glad you're here for the wedding." She kissed his cheek.

"Wouldn't miss it for the world."

"I love you, big brother, I love having you here for as long as you can stay."

"You only want me here to keep Mom out of your way."

"That too." She sat back with a grin on her face. "I mean it, though. I miss it when you're not around. Always have."

Guilt crept into his mind and heart. While he was overseas, he'd missed more than he ever wanted to admit to himself.

"I missed you when I was…." He couldn't find the words to use, so instead he shrugged.

"Hey." Kaitlin punched him in the arm. "Stop that!"

Nick lowered his head, resisting the urge to say sorry.

She patted his knee and then got to her feet. "Come on." She held out her hand.

"Where are we going?" He took her hand and stood.

"We are going to get a drink, and I'm going to introduce you to my gorgeous fiancé." She smiled brightly.

"I've seen photos, you know. Even talked to him by email."

"He's sexier in the flesh," she teased. "But he's totally straight, okay, so no flirting."

Nick poked her side. "I'll try. Okay. Just give me five to change my shirt."

Kaitlin kissed him on the cheek before leaving the room.

With a sigh, Nick pulled his phone from his jacket pocket, scrolled to his text messages, and selected Cameron's thread.

*Miss you already*, he typed, then hit Send.

Kaitlin waited at the bottom of the stairs, bundled up in a thick green winter coat, her gloves and beanie an especially vibrant shade of neon pink.

He couldn't help himself as big brother teasing just spilling from his lips. "I'm blind!" he cried and clamped his hands over his eyes.

"Ass," Kaitlin said without heat and poked him. "Hurry up. I need wine."

"You always need wine." Nick pulled on his own coat, rummaging for gloves and instead finding a receipt for Mount Rushmore in the pocket. He glanced at it briefly before pushing it back in to keep it safe. The memories of that day—the blue skies, the walking, the photographs— were enough to make him smile. Kaitlin tossed him some gloves (thankfully a sedate navy) and a matching beanie.

His cell vibrated, but his gloved hands were too clumsy to pick up the phone and see whether it was Cameron answering his message. Nick wanted it to be him, wanted to read the message, but he knew he'd have to wait until he reached the familiar Stars Bar at the end of the street.

His nose was ice cold by the time they reached the bar; winter was gripping Vermont hard and not letting go. Snowdrifts were already four feet high at the side of the road, and more fell from the leaden skies. They burst into the bar, huffing at the cold. The prickle of heat on Nick's skin was a welcome sensation.

Coats off, they went in. Nick stood back as a tall man swept Kaitlin into a hug; her feet left the ground and she wrapped her arms around his neck. Nick took the time to look objectively at the man who had his sister's heart. He was taller than Nick, probably six four or so, in jeans and a white sweatshirt. His hair was wheat blond, and he was holding Kaitlin as if she were the most precious thing in the world.

So, this Jamie guy was nicely put together—not that Nick could see much of his face as he'd buried it in Kaitlin's hair. Then Jamie lowered Kaitlin to the floor, and hand in hand they stopped in front of Nick. Jamie was good-looking, his eyes a bright blue, his mouth curved in a ready smile, and he extended a hand to Nick.

"Jamie Drake," he said with confidence.

Nick took his hand and shook it firmly. "Nick."

They assessed each other, but Nick didn't see fear or concern in Jamie's face. Just determination, as if he was ready for Nick not to like him but felt he could handle that.

"Beer?" Jamie asked.

Beer sounded good, and so after the three of them got their beers and found a spot near the pool table, they got down to the details.

"So, what is it you do?" Nick asked, getting the first question in quickly.

"I'm a teacher. Math and Physics, so you never have to

worry about how I can support Kaitlin when we start a family."

"I wasn't worried," Nick lied. Of course he was worried. Kaitlin was his sister and her well-being was the very thing that concerned him; it was part of his job description.

"So," Jamie said. "Kaitlin says you were a Marine."

Nick nodded.

"Thank you for your service," Jamie said very seriously, his hand extended again.

Nick shook the hand and inclined his head, hoping that would be the end of it. He wanted to talk about Jamie and Kaitlin, not about himself. "Tell me about the wedding." That had to be a safe subject.

Jamie leaned in conspiratorially with a grin. "You think your mom is bad, you should meet your sister, Bridezilla."

Which earned him a punch on the arm and a scowl from Kaitlin. But none of it was serious, and Nick lost himself in discussions about venues and colors and plans.

The warmth of knowing he had a message from Cameron on his phone was enough to have him smiling at inappropriate times in the conversation, which in turn had Kaitlin looking at him with a fond smile on her face.

She was sappy.

Hell, *he* was sappy. Love clearly did that for people.

And Jamie? He was a nice, confident guy who clearly loved Kaitlin and wanted to promise her the world. Nick couldn't ask for anything more.

## Chapter Eighteen

CAMERON PULLED UP OUTSIDE THE SHERIDAN HOUSE AND honked, grinning when Nick appeared almost immediately, as if he'd been waiting.

He half-jogged down the snowy path and slid to a stop by the car, climbed in, and within seconds had his cold hands on Cameron's face and was kissing him.

Cameron gave as good as he got, leaning into the kiss and reminding himself of the taste of Nick. *Intoxicating.* "Wow," he said when they finally separated. "That was some welcome."

Nick pressed one final soft kiss to his mouth. "Didn't want things to be awkward. I want to kiss you. I want you, so I thought I'd make it obvious."

The journey to Angelo's Italian restaurant wasn't more than five minutes, but during that time, even though they were quiet by necessity because of the snow, Nick had his hand on Cameron's leg as though he never wanted to stop touching him.

They parked, stole another kiss, and walked into the

restaurant, where a waiter showed them to their table right in the back, with a view of the spotlighted patio. Snow danced in the soft glow, and everything was covered with a layer of white.

Angelo's was the kind of place where you brought a lover, and Cameron knew he'd done the right thing.

"I missed you," he said. "I know I said that in every text, but I really did." He paused, aware he'd put the ball firmly in Nick's court.

"I missed you too." Nick reached over to take his hand. "I know we need to talk, but I don't like talking. We have to cover the logistics of our relationship, and I get that. But, I *am* coming back to Seattle with you, and I *will* find a job and get my qualifications, and we *will* get a place together."

Cameron sat back in his chair. He wanted exactly the same thing, but he honestly thought there would be a lot more talking to get to that point. "You decided all that for us?" he teased.

Nick looked uncertain, but only for a moment, and then the confident Marine was front and center again. "Yep. You want to disagree?"

God, he sounded cocky, and Cameron wanted so badly to tease him and draw this out. But he couldn't; there would be time for teasing later. "No disagreement here. There is one big decision, though, that we need to hash out."

Nick leaned in, his expression serious and focused, his dark gaze fixed on Cameron. "Go on." He didn't sound worried, just ready to argue his position.

"Are we driving back or getting a plane?"

Nick chuckled. "The car's a rental, right?"

"Yep."

"There somewhere we can return the car over here?"

"Yep," Cameron said again.

"Plane, then. I'm too impatient to have to wait to start our lives together." Nick sat back, as if all the decisions had been made, but there was one more thing that Cameron wanted to cover after they'd ordered.

So, they talked about the wedding for a while. About Nick and Kaitlin's mom, who had sat them down last night and talked about how her babies were growing up and how life moved on.

"…And then she started to cry," Nick said, horror in his voice. "And I didn't know what to say or do."

"Mom-crying is a bad one," Cameron agreed. God knew he'd seen enough of it when he'd been ill, and his mom still teared up sometimes when she saw him. Had done just the other night when he'd gotten home from dropping Nick.

Nick continued. "Then she went on about Jill from the salon, whose cousin's son—or something like that—was posted overseas and didn't make it back. Then she cried again and wouldn't let go of my hand. When you sign up, because there's no way that you can't if it's in you—" He paused, and Cameron gripped his hand tight.

Making the decision to sign up wasn't one that anybody made lightly, he was sure of that. "What?" he prompted when Nick had been quiet for the longest time.

Nick sighed. "You sign up for your country, for your family, but it's not always you that has to be the strong one, but the people who love you. They have to live with your decisions as well."

Cameron agreed. His cancer as a kid was tough on

him, changed him as a child and an adult, screwed with his head and made him scared to commit to anything. But his mom? She blamed herself and would have died for him. Cancer, like war, was soul-destroying.

"And then I made her smile," Nick said, "by telling her I'd fallen in love with you. She just started crying all over again after that. Something about wanting her kids to be happy."

"Then what happened?"

"She gave me a small box and said I should think about what I wanted to do with the contents."

The music changed, soft carols piping into the warmth of the restaurant, reminding Cameron of the magic of the season. Somehow he knew Nick's story would be something special. "What was in the box?"

Nick dropped his gaze to the table. Cameron waited. He wasn't going to ask again. Clearly something important was happening, and Nick needed the time-to-process thing. Had Nick even opened the box? *Damn, I should have asked that first.*

"It was my grandfather's. I'll show you," Nick finally reached into the pocket of his jeans, pulling out a small wooden box no bigger than a few inches square. He opened it, but Cameron still couldn't see what was inside. Maybe a medal or something? Nick's family had a history of service in other generations, and Cameron was sure his grandfather had also been a Marine.

Then, Nick cleared his throat and turned the box to face Cameron, revealing a heavy silver-colored ring, a twist of strands, worn with age.

"This is for you," Nick said. "If you want it."

Cameron looked at the ring in its bed of aged silk, at

the way the Christmas lights reflected in the surface of the metal. "What is it?" he asked.

He meant a lot of things. *Why a ring? Are you asking me to wear it? Do you want to give that to me as a thank you? Or as a promise?*

"It's a ring," Nick explained patiently. "Or, more exactly, it's the ring my Granny Kat gave to my grandfather as a wedding ring, when it wasn't even fashionable for husbands to wear a ring. Mom said the story was that when he left her to go overseas, that he took the ring, and he wore it on a chain around his neck. It was his good-luck charm, his wedding ring."

Cameron felt the weight of history and reached for the ring before stopping, his fingers a breath from touching it. "But," he began softly, "what is it?"

"I won't ask you now," Nick said. "But when we're settled, and I have a job, and you know what you're doing, and we have a place... maybe... we could make this permanent. We could get married."

Cameron locked his gaze with Nick's, uncertain of the words to say, seeing the flicker of worry in Nick's expression. *Married?* Only a week ago he'd thought he could be dying again, desperately wanting to grip hold of every minute and not let go. Things were different now. He was different. His future as uncertain as the next man's, but there was still the specter of cancer that would always haunt him.

The uncertainty in Nick's face became something else: a brash confidence.

"I take it that's a yes, then?" he said, giving Cameron time to say no. "Because I love you, and you're my future, and I thank whoever is listening every day that I have you in my life for however long we can have."

And there it was, summed up in a few words, and Cameron knew exactly what he was going to say.

"Yes. Let's get married."

CAMERON WASN'T SITTING with Nick for the service. Nick was up the front with the bridal party, Cameron in the middle on the bride's side. He had caught a glimpse of Nick in the general chaos of arrival, but since then, nothing.

The wedding was beautiful; there was no better word for it. All those adjectives about weddings rang true. Kaitlin was beautiful and couldn't stop smiling, and Jamie, handsome in his suit, looked like the proudest man in the room as they exchanged their vows.

The bridal procession was slow, and for the longest time, Nick and Cameron were only a foot apart, and it was all that Cameron could do not to reach over and grasp Nick and kiss him, however inappropriate it might be to steal the bride's thunder.

Last night he had said yes to Nick, had promised that they would make this thing work between them, and right then all Cameron wanted to do was grab Nick and hold him close.

They finally had a few moments to themselves when the bride and groom had left for their honeymoon and the dancing was dying down.

In the middle of a heated kiss, Cameron knew one thing for certain: however long forever was, he would spend it with Nick.

# Epilogue

## ONE YEAR LATER

THE CAR BROKE DOWN JUST OUTSIDE FROSTY HOLLOW.

Instead of hiring a car that was mechanically sound, as Nick had suggested, Cameron had made the decision to buy an old car, a red '67 Ford Mustang, and said that if they broke down, Nick could fix it.

Because that was what Nick did for a living now: half his time working for the studio, the other half on vintage restorations. So, the whole road trip from Seattle was no kind of holiday for Nick. Not that he really minded, because hell, he loved this car, and he loved Cameron.

"That doesn't mean I want to spend our road trip fixing the damn thing" was all he'd said when he first saw the Mustang. And now, on the quiet back road into Frosty Hollow, the car had finally given up the ghost. Literally only five minutes' drive from Kaitlin's house. He wanted to say "I told you so," but he took one look at Cameron's regretful expression, and something melted inside him.

So what if the car had broken down? They were close to home. So what if the fields were white with snow? At least it wasn't snowing now. So what if walking the rest of the way meant hauling cases and a hundred gifts for their new niece, Leanne, born only a few weeks before?

"I'm not carrying the rabbit," Nick said as he popped the hood.

The battery wasn't charging and the oil leak had become an oil rush by the look of it. If they let the engine cool, they could very well make it to town. Said rabbit was four feet tall and took up half the trunk.

"I'm telling your niece you wouldn't bring her rabbit," Cameron teased, walking around to lean against the car. "Can you fix it?"

Nick could fix it, easily, if he had access to a pit, his tools, and maybe an entire new engine. He didn't say that. Instead, he fished out his phone and thumbed to his sister's number. She answered on the first ring; in the background a baby was crying.

"Hey," she said, apparently unfazed by the noise. "How long now?"

"Small problem," Nick began. He was going to explain about how this was all Cameron's fault, teasingly of course, but Cameron crowded into his space and linked his hands behind Nick's neck. "Can one of you come pick us up? We're up by the McGregors' place."

The phone muffled and Nick could hear talking.

Then Kaitlin was back. "Jamie will be with you in five. He'll borrow a tow truck."

"Thanks, sis."

He ended the call. "Five minutes," he repeated to Cameron, who smiled up at him and then kissed him gently.

Night was drawing in, a smudge of light on the horizon

all that remained of the day, and the dark silhouettes of trees marked the edge of town. He and Cameron were wrapped up in coats, gloves, beanies, and each other.

A whole year like this, and Nick never grew tired of the taste of Cameron or having him in his life.

The road to Frosty Hollow might have stopped a little short this time, but right here with Cameron in his arms, he didn't care.

Wherever Cameron was, Nick knew one thing...

He was home.

## Sapphire Cay

### Sapphire Cay

1. Follow the Sun
2. Under the Sun
3. Chase The Sun
4. Christmas In The Sun
5. Capture The Sun
6. Forever In The Sun

# Boyfriends for Hire

## Boyfriends For Hire

1. <u>Darcy</u>
2. <u>Kaden</u>
3. Gideon
4. Jared
5. Felix
6. Caleb

## Standalone Christmas

- <u>The Road to Frosty Hollow</u>

# Meet RJ Scott

RJ discovered romance in books at a very young age and realized that if there wasn't romance on the page, she could create it in her head. With over one hundred and fifty books published, she is a full time author of gay romance.

She lives and works out of her home in the beautiful English countryside, spends her spare time reading, watching films, and enjoying time with her family.

The last time she had a week's break from writing she didn't like it one little bit and has yet to meet a box of chocolates she couldn't defeat.

www.rjscott.co.uk | rj@rjscott.co.uk

**NEWSLETTER - rjscott.co.uk/rjnews**

facebook.com/author.rjscott

instagram.com/rjscott_author

amazon.com/author/rj-scott

bookbub.com/authors/rj-scott

goodreads.com/rjscott

patreon.com/RJScott

## Meet Meredith Russell

Meredith Russell lives in the heart of England. An avid fan of many story genres, she enjoys nothing less than a happy ending. She believes in heroes and romance and strives to reflect this in her writing. Sharing her imagination and passion for stories and characters is a dream Meredith is excited to turn into reality.

www.meredithrussell.co.uk
meredithrussell666@gmail.com

 facebook.com/meredithrussellauthor

 x.com/MeredithRAuthor

 instagram.com/miss_meredith_r

www.ingramcontent.com/pod-product-compliance
Lightning Source LLC
Chambersburg PA
CBHW060440180626
46817CB00007B/2905